Innocent until proven guilty...

Janelle sat in a hardbacked chair, a Formica table in front of her. She could almost see the layers of guilt on the table and feel them beneath her on the chair, accumulated over the years by criminals who had been there before her.

The air inside the building was stifling. A ceiling fan stirred the dust and smoke, but brought no relief. At least she was no longer handcuffed, and she tried to convince herself that she had no idea why she'd been arrested. It was simply a ghastly mistake.

Then the policeman came forward to take her fingerprints....

ABOUT THE AUTHOR

Andrea Davidson lives in Houston with her
husband and two children. She began her
writing career with the American Medical
Association in Chicago. Since then she
has written several Harlequin American
Romances. Andrea has traveled extensively
in foreign countries and incorporates
the exotic background of Athens in
Out from the Shadows, her second Intrigue.

Books by Andrea Davidson

HARLEQUIN INTRIGUE
25–A SIREN'S LURE

HARLEQUIN AMERICAN ROMANCE
  1–THE GOLDEN CAGE
 16–MUSIC IN THE NIGHT
 21–UNTAMED POSSESSION
 45–TREASURES OF THE HEART
122–AN UNEXPECTED GIFT

These books may be available at your local bookseller.

Don't miss any of our special offers. Write to us at the
following address for information on our newest releases.

Harlequin Reader Service
901 Fuhrmann Blvd., P.O. Box 1397, Buffalo, NY   14240
Canadian address: P.O. Box 2800, Postal Station A,
5170 Yonge St., Willowdale, Ont.   M2N 6J3

OUT FROM THE SHADOWS

ANDREA DAVIDSON

Harlequin Books

TORONTO • NEW YORK • LONDON
AMSTERDAM • PARIS • SYDNEY • HAMBURG
STOCKHOLM • ATHENS • TOKYO • MILAN

Harlequin Intrigue edition published May 1986

ISBN 0-373-22041-3

Prologue

An Austrian-made, double-action, 9 mm semi-automatic was pointed at him. A powerful, accurate handgun. The young Greek man with the dark brooding eyes knew that he was looking squarely into the face of death, but somehow there was nothing very profound about it. He was mildly interested in the fact that the bullet would enter his body in a spiral, shattering flesh and bone and living tissue before it exited through the other side. And he was vaguely surprised that he hadn't anticipated it.

"I should have known," Nikos said to the man holding the gun. His voice held an uncustomary tremble.

"Yes, you should have."

Nikos glanced toward the bedroom window. Springtime in Athens. His favorite time of year. He was sweating as if it was July. Taking one step backward, he said, "It gains you nothing, you know. You still do not have the coin." A strange laugh came from his throat. "She has it."

The man with the gun did not laugh. But he was amused as he watched Nikos backing away. "Yes, and she will give it to me. I will see to that."

Nikos glanced down at the scribbled note in his hand. "And then you will kill her?"

"Yes."

Nikos thought briefly of the woman, but his thoughts held no sympathy, no regrets. Her death was her own problem. "Things could have been different. We could have made a deal. It doesn't have to be this way."

"If only you had it here, Nikos. If only you hadn't given it to the girl." The gunman shrugged. "You knew the risks in this little game of yours. You accepted them without question." A sneer pulled at his face. "But since you cannot give me what I want, you are like a scourge to me. And like all other pestilences, you must be rubbed out."

The Greek had thought he had planned it out so carefully. He had the evidence he needed to destroy them all. Now it was he who was to be destroyed, eliminated by a man he'd believed he could trust.

The clicking sound of the gun's safety was magnified in the room. He heard a loud pop, shuddered once in hot convulsive pain, then felt no more.

The man with the gun watched him crumple to the floor and frowned. He was mildly disappointed. He had expected more of a struggle, had hoped to hear Nikos plead for his life, had wanted to see him cry. His going without a whimper had taken all the fun out of it.

Shrugging, he pulled a handkerchief from his pocket and carefully wiped the gun clean of all prints, then dropped it to the rug.

He glanced around to make sure he had forgotten nothing. It was a man's bedroom, with furnishings and colors designed for a man's taste. Dark woods, a large bureau, a neutral bedspread in a nubby weave, paintings of sailboats and white mountain landscapes. But it was the little things—the basket of makeup on top of the bureau, the brushes and combs on the bathroom vanity, the tailored suits and dresses hanging in the closet alongside the loosely shaped blouses and jeans—that said a woman lived there now. A woman who lived alone. The one who would give him what he had come for. He glanced through the window and was irritated to see that the apartment building across the street blocked all view of the Acropolis. He hated progress.

Moving to the doorway, he stopped once to smile down at the body, then walked downstairs into the living room. He picked up the telephone and dialed. The call did not go through, so he patiently tried again.

"I believe someone has been shot," he said to the police officer who answered. "In the home of Professor Loukas Goulandris in Kolonaki. Number Seven. I was walking by. I heard the gunshot. A young woman ran out of the house—American, I believe.... Yes, of course I will wait for the police to get here."

He hung up the phone, then carefully wiped it with the handkerchief from his pocket. After glancing toward the stairway once more, he walked through the foyer, out the front door and down the sidewalk, losing himself within minutes in the crowded hustle-bustle of Syntagma Square.

Chapter One

The first sensation that escaped was instinctive and physical. She was going to be sick. Violently so.

Janelle clutched the thick, carved doorcasing that had faded through the years to a dull gray, clutched it as the sickness clawed its way painfully into her stomach, her lungs, her throat. She stared vacantly at the thick pool of blood that was mingling with the rug's floral border, staining the roses an even darker and more vivid red. Horrified, she moved her eyes along the crimson line to where more blood had splattered, like a child's first attempt at art, onto the white wall. Her focus was drawn back hypnotically and involuntarily to the rug. She tried not to let the image connect or mold itself into reality. She tried to concentrate on anything except that crumpled body lying face-down on the floor of her bedroom. Nikos's body.

There was a sound in the back of her throat, but she didn't recognize it. Her skin was clammy, and she felt as if something vital were oozing from the marrow of her bones, leaving her limp and faint. She wondered vaguely if the men standing there would catch her if her knees gave way.

At the thought, she jerked and looked over at their blue-gray uniforms. They were not just men. They were the local gendarmerie. Policemen. One of them pinched a gun at the tip of the barrel as if not wanting to smudge prints. And all three of them were staring at her in silence. Disbelief edged closer to hysteria as she heard another noise come from her throat. She sensed that they were trying to tell her something, but exactly what it was seemed suspended in the irrational gray haze of the moment.

Through the subliminal fog she watched the policemen step over the body and move toward her, speaking words she could not understand.

Janelle had come to Greece expecting springtime in the Aegean, where the Olympian gods smiled down on the islands with sunshine and warm breezes. In this moment, however, there was neither sunshine nor warmth. Today the gods were not smiling.

The men were still speaking to her, yet Janelle could only stare back at them with blank eyes. She spoke five languages fluently, but Greek was not one of them. Since the ambassador had become ill and vacated his post, the deputy chief of mission, acting as chargé d'affaires, had been in a hurry to fill the position of staff assistant. And because of Janelle's facility with languages, her high scores on the foreign service exam and her impressive parentage, she had been assigned to Athens with the provision that she learn Greek within a couple of months.

Tomorrow she would have been in Greece for exactly one week.

The policemen reached out for her. She was turned around, and her hands were yanked roughly behind

her back. She felt the cold metal cuffs slip around her
wrists, heard the click of the lock snap into place.

Ironically, the language barrier lifted like a gossa-
mer veil to expose the stark face beneath. Not a thread
of ambiguity was left dangling.

Janelle now understood Greek perfectly.

CIGARS WERE PASSED AROUND the heavy oak table. A
tall, dark Greek, wearing baggy white pants and a
black tunic shirt, walked from chair to chair, holding
the gold lighter beneath the tip of each imported
Monte Cruz. All talk would be suspended until he left
the room and closed the door behind him.

Alec Hayden forcefully stilled the impatient tap-
ping of his foot, took a deep drag on the cigar, leaned
back in his leather chair and wished like hell this whole
ludicrous affair was over and done with. Whoever
said, "If you don't have anything to do, do it with
style," was obviously referring to the conference calls
of James Eddington Bluminfeld, the American chargé
d'affaires to Greece. The chargé's delicate constitu-
tion was advertised by the number of pills he had just
swallowed. Thin and effeminate, he looked ridicu-
lously small with that huge cigar. But James Bluminfeld firmly believed that pomposity was the seat of
bureaucratic power, and with his recently obtained
status as head of the embassy, he had elevated that seat
to nothing less than a throne.

While Alec watched the swarthy Greek servant
move around the table, he mentally tallied up the tax-
payers' cost for this little powwow. Five men at me-
dium-to-high five-figure salaries and another at a
slightly lower level—that would be about $450 for a
two-hour meeting. Then there was the pittance in

drachmas paid to the Greek and, of course, $75 for the cigars.

Such a waste of time and money. Everything that needed to be said had been covered in the report— eighty pages of double-spaced black script that no one would ever read. Thirty-five dollars for the secretary who typed the report; eight dollars for the typewriter use, ribbon and paper; sixty dollars for the Cross pens and pads of paper in front of each man.

And what added even more of a carnival atmosphere to the meeting was that the report was nothing more than a smoke screen. No one at the table knew the real reason that Alec had come to Greece. And no one was going to have any suspicions, either, not if he could help it.

His narrowed gaze swept around the table, stopping first on Frank Osborn, the chief of security for the embassy. Short and stocky, with a paunch that would have been stiff competition for any sumo wrestler, Frank carried his weight and his responsibilities with the gravity of a sheriff in Dodge City. He even dressed the part, in boots and suits with Western stitching. Alec had first met him when Osborn was head of security at the embassy in Tripoli. But since the severance of diplomatic relations between the United States and Libya, he had taken over the security staff in Athens.

Sitting next to Frank was Dimitris Heraki, a Greek-American who served as liaison and agent between American business executives or congressional delegates and the various ministries of the Greek government. He was a nervous man who continually licked his lips and sniffed. Alec had suspected for quite some

time that Dimitris was a heavy cocaine user, a habit
that required a steady supply of cash.

Besides Bluminfeld, Osborn and Dimitris Heraki,
there was a staff assistant and a Yale law student who
was acting as aide to some congressman.

"Now..." Bluminfeld began in a watered-down
tone of voice that grated on Alec's nerves. He paused
to realign the papers and pens in front of him, shift his
glass of water—Waterford crystal at $45 a glass—and
after giving his territory the once-over to make certain everything was in its rightful slot, he began again.
"Now, as you all know, we have exactly two months
before the congressional delegation arrives in Athinai."

Athinai. Alec tried not to snort. Who the hell was
Bluminfeld hoping to impress anyway? Surely not that
green kid from Yale in the oversize Hickey Freeman
suit.

"Since you have met Alec Hayden, I will dispense
with the introductions. In cases like this where dignitaries will be visiting a foreign country, it is custom-
ary for the State Department to send someone to beef
up security. That they decided to send Alec is...rather
exceptional. He is, as you all know, the best in the
business. This is no reflection on you, of course,
Frank. Everyone knows what a tremendous job you
do here as chief of security."

Frank smiled thinly at the chargé, then exchanged
a quick conspiratorial wink with Alec.

"Anyway," Bluminfeld continued, "Alec has provided us with a detailed report of the necessary security checks, for which we are most grateful." He laid
his hand on top of the bound report, slim fingers
spread and slightly curled under. This was as close as

he would ever get to opening the report and reading it.
"And now, Alec, if you would be so kind as to fill us
in on your recommendations."

Alec spun the cigar in the crystal ashtray, tapering
the ashes and giving himself the necessary space to
cloak his disgust. He wasn't going to stand up and tell
Bluminfeld to stuff it. He really wasn't. He was going
to remain calm and civilized. But damn, the chargé
was almost more than he could bear. Alec had been on
the go since the first of April. Tel Aviv, Riyadh, Cairo.
And now this.

Athens had been an unexpected stopover. A problem had arisen, and he had to take care of it. He had
decided to use the impending congressional visit as a
perfect excuse for his presence on the scene. Now if he
could just do what he was there to do and cut through
all this backwater bureaucratic bilge, he'd feel a hell
of a lot better.

He took a deep breath and opened his mouth to begin.

"Uh, Alec," Bluminfeld interrupted. "Would you
mind standing so we could see and hear you better?"

Alec stared at the chargé, then let his gaze circle the
table. Only five people were there besides himself.
They were sitting at a round table, for God's sake—
with ringside seats! Now who the hell couldn't see
him?

He knew most of the political games; he had been
forced to play them off and on for quite a few years
now. The chargé wanted it on record that, no matter
who had the floor, he, James Eddington Bluminfeld,
was in command. Oh, yes, Hayden knew the games.
Backward and forward. But he played them only when
they suited him.

"Nope," he said, not even looking at Bluminfeld. "I'll sit." He leaned back deliberately in his chair, picked up the cigar, clamped his teeth on it and spoke around it. "I've outlined everything in the report, so it might be a good idea if you all read it and familiarized yourselves with it." He removed the cigar from his lips and stared pointedly at Bluminfeld before looking back at the others. "I don't need to tell any of you how much more important security has become at our embassies in the past couple of years. In some locales more than in others, of course. And Frank has done a hell of a job here. So," he said, suppressing a big yawn, "there are only a few things that need to be added for the congressional visit. Actually, there are three steps to be followed and—oh, hell, what now!" He glared irritably at the phone in front of the chargé.

Bluminfeld picked it up before the second ring and embellished his words with little grace notes that slipped between each syllable. "Didn't I say we did not want to be disturbed, Sarah? Didn't I?" After a substantial pause, he said, "Oh. When? Where?" There was another pause. "No, the vice-consul is on leave. Dimitris is taking care of those types of cases. Tell the lieutenant we will handle it."

Before Bluminfeld could replace the phone, Dimitris was leaning forward in his seat, his eyes flashing uncomfortably from one person to the next before centering on the surface of the table just in front of the chargé. "There is a problem?"

Bluminfeld picked up his glass of water and wiped the circle of condensation from the table with his initialed handkerchief. He sighed. "It seems that one of our junior staff assistants has gotten herself arrested."

Dimitris frowned and sniffed loudly. "Who is it?"

"Janelle Lindsey."

"Hmm," Frank Osborn mused, tipping back his chair and hooking his hands behind his head in an unflappable pose. "You'd think she'd know enough to show them her ID."

"Diplomatic immunity won't hold on this one, I'm afraid." Bluminfeld cleared his throat a few times, then reached into his coat pocket and extracted a new packet of pills. After downing them with the water, he used his handkerchief to wipe both his mouth and the glass before he set the Waterford crystal on the table. "This bloody pollution is going to be the death of us all yet."

The front legs of Frank's chair hit the floor. "It occurs to me that Alec might be interested in this little gal's problem."

Alec was just snapping his briefcase shut and getting ready to go. "No, thanks," he said quickly. "I'm scheduled out of here this afternoon."

"That's right." Bluminfeld nodded. "And I think we can handle these minor matters without the State Department getting involved."

"Minor matter!" Frank sputtered. "Thomas Lindsey's daughter?"

Alec's head jerked toward the chargé. "Ambassador Lindsey's daughter?"

"Former ambassador," Bluminfeld corrected. "Really, now, Dimitris is quite capable of handling this in the vice-consul's absence. Isn't that correct, Dimitris?"

"But of course," Dimitris replied, his mouth a tight, hard line. This was his chance to make a move up the ladder. He didn't need some big shot from the

State Department breathing down his neck. He could handle the situation on his own. And he knew that Bluminfeld felt the same way. Nobody wanted interference from State.

"Yeah, but international law is Hayden's specialty," Frank argued. "And we aren't just talking about any old government servant here."

"I am scheduled out of Athens this afternoon," Alec repeated, but his tone and posture reflected a certain resignation. Dammit! The last thing he wanted to do was to deal with the gendarmerie over some junior consulate official who was stupid enough to get herself arrested. But the arrest of a former ambassador's daughter—especially an ambassador of Lindsey's status—would not be taken lightly by the department. They would expect him at least to look into the situation.

He didn't have to be in Ankara until tomorrow afternoon, but he had planned to have one whole day to himself in Antalya, doing nothing more significant than lying on the beach next to some of those gorgeous German girls who flocked to the resorts there. He glanced at Bluminfeld and sighed. "I'm not here to step on anyone's toes, James. But you know as well as I do that I should talk to her and to the authorities, too. If it's a minor offense, I'll turn it over to Dimitris. Still, I'd better check it out."

Bluminfeld drummed his fingertips on the table in a display of irritation. "All right, Hayden, deal with the authorities on this, if you must. But please, wrap it up quickly and neatly. And no fanfare. What we don't need now is to have this—this affair spread around the political community."

Alec stubbed out his cigar. "I'll make it quick. I'm sure I'll be out of your hair by nightfall. What have they got her on anyway, some trumped-up drug charge?"

A reluctant James Eddington Bluminfeld picked up his glass of water and lifted it to his lips, staring at Alec over the rim. "Murder."

Chapter Two

If Janelle had heard about this from someone, she would have said it could happen only in the movies. But it was real. And it was happening to her now. She sat in a straight-backed chair, a wide Formica table in front of her. She could almost see the layers of guilt on the table and feel them beneath her on the chair, piled one on top of the other over the years by criminals who had been there before her.

The air inside the building was stifling. A ceiling fan was whirring above, but all it did was stir up the smoke and dust around her until she thought she would pass out. At least, thank heaven, she was no longer handcuffed. But she had no idea how long she had been sitting there or how much longer she would have to stay.

She tried to convince herself that she also had no idea why she'd been arrested.

The day had begun nicely, with a sultry April breeze wafting in from the Aegean, blowing away some of the noxious smog that increasingly clogged Athens's heart and breath. Even in the gray megalopolis, there were signs everywhere that it was spring. Silvery-green olive trees graced broad avenues, and the parks were brilliant with tiny pink almond blossoms.

Janelle had left the embassy around ten so that she would have time to do some shopping before she had lunch in Syntagma Square, the social center of the city. Located midway between the hills of the Acropolis and Lykavitos, Syntagma was bordered by hotels, travel agencies and *zaharoplastias*—those ubiquitous little sweetshops that had replaced the more traditional *kafenios* in modern Athens.

She had carried a sandwich in a sack as she made the rounds of several shops, but she was going to buy a piece of cake and a cool drink at a favorite sweetshop called Floka's. The typical workday in Athens began at six-thirty in the morning and lasted until two-thirty in the afternoon, when the Greeks went home for big meals and for two hours' sleep. They got up at six-thirty, took showers then went out again for several more hours' work or play before finally retiring sometime after midnight.

The American diplomatic community did not follow that routine. Work hours for Janelle were from eight to five, with a lunch break in between. But that morning she had left the embassy early to go shopping. Funny, she couldn't even remember if she had bought anything. She did remember that after she'd left one of the shops, she had strolled through Zapio Gardens. The springtime profusion of flowers and the cool shade of the orange trees had enticed her to take the leisurely walk that would give her a good view of the Acropolis. But for some reason, before she had reached Syntagma she'd turned and headed north through the park, slipped down a shady alleyway, then walked a few blocks through Kolonaki. Situated on the northern slope of Mount Lykavitos, Kolonaki was the fashionable residential quarter for prominent Greek businessmen and foreign diplomats. Janelle had been assigned to live in the house of Professor Loukas Goulandris, a wealthy Greek effendi who had lent his property to the United States government while he was in America on sabbatical from the university.

She couldn't remember now why she had decided to go home instead of going to the square for lunch. There must have been a reason. Maybe she had forgotten to take something to work, or perhaps she had wanted to do something at the house. But now she could not remember what that something was.

She squeezed her eyes shut to hold the fear at bay. Nikos was dead. Murdered in her house. She stared down at her clenched hands and prayed silently. *Please let it be a bad dream. Please let me wake up soon.*

This post with the embassy had seemed like an oasis at the end of a long, dry road. She had worked toward it for many years and had invested nearly all of her emotional energy to achieve her goal. This was what she had waited for, the chance to prove to everyone that she could do it, that she was indeed Thomas Lindsey's daughter. She had gotten the grades, the postgraduate degree, the references, and had passed the five-hour foreign-service entrance exam with flying colors. And because her father had been a decorated Korean War veteran and had served as ambassador to three embassies during his illustrious career, Janelle had not been overlooked for what was considered in the trade to be a cushy post—the American Embassy in Greece.

Cushy post....

An image of Nikos's lifeless body lying on the floor flashed before her eyes, and she didn't know whether to cry again or to throw up.

It was the sound of the voice from across the room that erased both options. Four policemen were clustered around a tall man with brown, windblown hair. Janelle had seen him earlier that morning at the embassy, pacing restlessly back and forth in the same expensive three-piece suit with his tie loosened and askew, as if he were being choked and couldn't wait to yank it off. She knew only that he was American.

When they had first brought her to the police station, she had somehow had the presence of mind to show them her government identification. Most likely, the reason for this man's visit was to straighten out the nightmarish nonsense and get her released.

She couldn't understand the conversation, because he was speaking in Greek. His voice was deep, his manner of speaking authoritative and superior, but with a measured quality, as if he was carefully considering each word before he said it. In contrast, the other men's voices sounded agitated and clipped, and they kept glancing at Janelle while they talked. As far as she knew, the American had not yet looked at her. She continued to watch him, wondering what he was saying and what effect his words were having.

After a few minutes two policemen walked over to her. Each of them grabbed one of her hands, turning them over and staring at the fingertips. Then, frowning, the officers spoke quickly back and forth. Janelle tried to pull her hands away, but the men held them tightly.

She looked up as the American approached and she tried, once again unsuccessfully, to pull her hands free.

He did nothing to stop the policemen; he just stood there and watched them.

Emotional pain and fatigue tightened into a hard ball of frustration. Janelle wanted to lash out and smash her fists into this man who surely was supposed to be there to help her.

"Tell them to leave me alone!" She yanked hard in another effort to free herself. "They have no right to do this!"

Alec Hayden said something in Greek to the men, but they did not release her hands.

She tried not to cry. "What are they doing?"

Hayden stood in front of the table and stared down at her. "Looking for prints."

"Prints?"

"They're looking to see if you have fingerprints."

A note of hysteria crept into her voice. "Well, of course I have fingerprints. Everyone has fingerprints!"

With a nod of their heads, the men finally released her hands and moved away. When they had gone, Alec sat down on the edge of the table and kept his eyes riveted on her face, his words cool and evenly spaced. "Your lover didn't."

Janelle stared back at him. She noticed that a few gray streaks wove through his hair. He could be somewhere in his early forties, yet his face was that of a younger man. But it was his eyes she focused on. They were like a key that opened the door to a man's heart and mind. They spoke where words often failed to communicate. And right now this man's eyes were frigid gray, insensitive and deadly serious.

"No fingerprints?"

He shook his head. "Removed. An intricate and painful process. Not your standard thief."

"Thief?" She was starting to sound like some sort of mynah bird, mimicking everything he said. But her mind would not yet work on any other level.

He didn't bother to answer her. Instead, he flipped on a tape recorder.

"It's hot in here," she said, barely managing to eke out the words.

His eyes never left her face. "It will probably get hotter."

That was exactly what she didn't want to hear. "Who are you?"

"Alec Hayden. I'm with the State Department."

She nodded slowly, grateful for at least one answer that didn't require interpretation. "You—you are going to get me out of here... aren't you?"

"If I can. It won't be easy."

Puzzlement was reflected on her face. "I—I don't understand what is happening. Or why I am here. Am I to be charged with something, Mr. Hayden?"

He regarded her for a long moment before answering. "The murder of Nikos Marinatos."

Dazed, she stared back at him, disbelief etched in every line of her face. It had been there all along, of course, on the surface of her thoughts ever since the police had handcuffed her and brought her to headquarters. Yes, she had known, and yet she had refused to believe, refused to let the horror form into a cohesive whole. It was too incredible, too utterly preposterous even to consider. She still could not accept the fact that Nikos was dead, much less that he had been murdered. And by her...?

"That's—I . . ." The thought got lost in the tumult swirling in her head, and a thin layer of moisture clouded her eyes. When she finally spoke, her voice was a frail whisper. "Why—why would I kill Nikos? I hardly knew him."

"Oh, come now, Miss Lindsey, you were sleeping with the man."

Although the words were uttered softly, the sting of Hayden's voice was like a slap across the face.

"Only—only once," she whispered defensively. Oh, no, she hadn't said that right at all! Of course she knew Nikos. What she'd meant was that he was a stranger to her, a man she did not understand.

Hayden took her words at face value. "Once, twice, two hundred times." He shrugged. "The point is that you knew him intimately."

"How did you know we were, uh, intimate?"

"You just told me."

"But you—you called him my lover."

"An educated guess. The security officer's file on you states that you were seen with him on several occasions. You've been carefully observed, Miss Lindsey. Standard operating procedure."

"It wasn't like that...really. We were just...friends, I guess you'd say. Acquaintances." Her voice cracked. Hayden appeared as if the explanation and any emotions she might have would be lost on him anyway, a fact emphasized by his next statement.

"He was murdered in your bedroom."

That, of course, was the bottom line. Nikos had been killed, and the authorities believed she had caused his death. "I didn't kill him, Mr. Hayden. You have to believe me. What possible reason could I have had for killing him?"

He observed her closely. "The police estimate the time of murder at eleven o'clock this morning. Where were you?"

"I—I was shopping."

"Do you have any sales receipts? Is there anyone— a shopkeeper, maybe—who could verify your alibi?"

Suddenly she remembered. She had been looking for a gift for her mother but had not found what she wanted in any of the shops. The reality of her dilemma hit her. Swallowing hard, she shook her head. "No.... But ... you didn't answer my question, Mr. Hayden. Why would I kill Nikos?"

"The police have their hunches. But they want to hear it from you."

"Hear what?" she cried, and several pairs of eyes focused on her from across the room.

"About your connection with him."

She looked at the State Department man in wonderment. His voice was so calm, so steady, his eyes an impersonal slate gray. They were talking about *murder* here. They were talking about her life! Didn't he realize that? "My connection with him..." she said lethargically. "You already know that we had a—a physical relationship."

Oh, dear, how could she have said that she hardly knew him? It was just that she couldn't even begin to explain that Nikos had represented her first brush with real freedom, her first spontaneous and reckless act. She had led a rather sheltered life. She had never been exposed to anyone like Nikos before, so she'd had no defense mechanisms to counter his relentless pursuit of her. He was different. She had felt unfettered. But after their one night of intimacy, his behavior toward her had changed for the worse. At the same time, her sanity had returned, forcing them into a strictly platonic relationship. During the past week she had come to realize that Nikos was a virtual stranger; he was also a man who frightened her. If only she had known how to defuse his power over her!

All of her life she had been a good girl. She had tried to please, to do what was right and what was expected of her. So how could this have happened? How could she have gotten involved with a man like Nikos, thereby jeopardizing everything she had ever planned and worked for? Moreover, how could she ever explain it so that Alec Hayden and the American government would understand? She took note of his closed expression as he towered over her, and she realized it would be futile even to try. "I had a—a brief relationship with him, Mr. Hayden. I hardly knew the man otherwise."

"Do you do that often?"

"Do I do what often?"

With his palm resting on the table, he leaned his weight into it and bent closer. "Do you often have physical relationships with men you hardly know?"

Her voice, when she finally found it, was thin and unsure. "I would say that's irrelevant to this case."

His eyes narrowed. "Maybe. Maybe not." He studied her hard. She was prettier than the picture in her file indicated, with smoky brown eyes that looked innocent but could be very deceptive. Her dark hair was pulled back into one long braid that hung down between her shoulder blades. A few tendrils had come loose and were clinging to the perspiration on her face. Her age was listed as twenty-seven, but right now she looked much younger. She was wearing a blue suit, very tailored, very proper, with a pale pink silk blouse that hinted at a looser, less brittle side to her personality.

Janelle's pale, slim hands were clasped on the table in front of her. She was hot and scared but was able, amazingly enough, to remain in control. In his book, that could mean one of several things. Either she was a true professional who could hold her own even when the going got rough, or she was still in a state of shock over her lover's death, unable to absorb what was happening any faster. Or—and this was the most likely possibility of all—she was as guilty as hell.

This case was not going to be easy to crack. But he would do it. She—or someone—had killed the man he had come to Greece to see. His real purpose for being in Athens was not to check on security at the embassy. Frank had that situation completely under control. Alec's help certainly wasn't needed, but that was merely his cover for meeting with Nikos Marinatos. Now the case he had intended to build was without a foundation. If this Lindsey woman was connected with Marinatos, then she must know something, anything that could help Alec find what he was after.

He opened the dossier in front of him.

"What is that?" she asked.

"Your file. I haven't yet had time to go over it very well."

"Why didn't James Bluminfeld come? I work for him."

Alec didn't look up from the file. "He asked me to handle it."

"I see." Janelle saw only too clearly. If the chargé didn't want to come to the police station and oversee her release, the reason could be twofold. Either he felt that Alec Hayden was quite capable of taking care of it, or he thought she was guilty of the crime as charged.

"Graduate of the University of Geneva," Alec mumbled, reading from the file. "Dual degree in Russian and French. A master's in world economics from Georgetown. No field experience ... no traffic tickets ... no affiliation with any organizations...."

Alec was impatiently flipping through the pages, frowning as if the file were incomplete, as if someone's life history could not possibly be contained in so few pages and with so few shortcomings. He obviously believed she had withheld information.

"I've never concealed anything from anyone, Mr. Hayden. I've had nothing happen to me that's worthy of secrecy. I have nothing to hide now."

He finally looked up at her. "That's good, Miss Lindsey," he said. "Because if you have anything of any kind buried or tucked away, I'm going to ferret it out. You will have no secrets from me, professional *or* personal. We're going to start with Nikos Marinatos." He held up a piece of paper. "And this."

When he had first come into the police station and she had heard his voice, she had assumed he was there to free her. He was to be the lifeboat amid this choppy, unpredictable sea into which she had fallen headlong. But now, as she stared up into the impenetrable wall of his face, she suspected that he was not there to save her at all. He was there to hang her.

She lowered her gaze and inspected the piece of paper he was holding out to her, but she didn't take it from him. She could read the one line written on it. "So."

"So," he echoed.

"So what is it?"

"It is obviously a message that was written to you."

"How do you figure that?"

"It was found in your bedroom."

"Someone has—has been going through my things?"

"You are a prime suspect in a murder case, Miss Lindsey. Your personal effects are now fair game. And yes, your house has been thoroughly searched."

With shaking fingers, she took the crumpled note from him and read it again, this time out loud. "'Don't give it up to anyone but Zafer—no matter what!'"

"Is that Marinatos's handwriting? And his signature?"

Janelle shook her head. "I—I don't know. I never saw him sign anything or—or write anything. I met him only a little more than a month ago."

"And this Zafer?"

"Zafer Demir. A friend of Nikos's."

Alec watched her for a few more seconds before saying, "The police will want to talk to him." He left the room and came back with a large bottle of water and two glasses. After pouring the water, he set one glass in front of her. "Now, where did you meet Marinatos?"

Janelle tipped the glass back and drank deeply. She needed food. She needed strength. She wondered what had happened to her sack lunch. "In Salzburg," she said.

"When was this?"

"It was about five weeks ago. I had finished all of my brush-up courses on European economics. I thought I was going to be assigned as an economics aide somewhere. I had just concluded all my interviews for different foreign service positions. And then I got word about the opening in Athens. I flew into Zurich from the States and took a train from there. I wasn't due here until the twentieth of this month, and I wanted to travel around a bit and visit an old roommate of mine who now lives in Salzburg. Sondra Patton Van Zant is her name,'' Janelle added quickly, figuring he would probably have asked that anyway. She hoped they wouldn't give her friend a hard time over this. Sondra had just gone through a bad divorce. She didn't need the police on her back right now.

''Go on.''

''Sondra had a party one night. There were maybe thirty-five people there. Nikos was one of them.''

''He was a friend of your roommate?''

Janelle shook her head. ''No. In fact...'' She paused, frowning. ''Sondra asked me if I knew who he had come with.'' Janelle shrugged. ''I guess she found out later or else decided that it didn't matter. You see, Sondra is sort of a free spirit. She throws these bashes, and whoever shows up is automatically a friend.''

Alec was studying her closely, as if each inflection of her voice and each flicker of her eye held some hidden meaning. ''And did you talk to Marinatos at this party?''

''Yes. He overheard that I was coming to Athens on a diplomatic assignment, and he seemed very interested. He asked me all about my job, what I would be doing, who I would be working with.''

''And what did you tell him?''

''Nothing much. I know better than that. In this day and age of foreign service, it's much safer to maintain a low profile." A bitter sound escaped from her throat. "Some low profile this is."

Alec took a drink of his water, settled into his chair and rested his elbows on the table. "So then what happened with Nikos?"

Janelle sighed. It would be nice to forget that she was in a sea of trouble unlike any she had ever known or imagined. But Alec Hayden wasn't about to let her forget. Not for a minute. She took another drink and set the glass down. "Nothing much that night. We just talked, and he said he was heading for Athens the next day."

"Athens was where he lived?"

"No, he is—he was from Macedonia, but he had business here."

"What kind of business?"

"He didn't say?"

"You didn't ask?"

"Well, as a matter of fact, I did. But now that I think about it, he always changed the subject. He was very..."

"Very what?"

She hesitated, afraid she was going to cry. "Charming," she whispered.

Charming. Alec tried to fit the pieces together in his head. Here was a woman who, by all accounts, did not have a single blemish on her record. Yet this same woman had entangled herself with the likes of Nikos Marinatos. The pieces didn't fit. He stopped the recorder to see how much tape was left, then clicked on the machine again. "Okay," he finally said, "then what?"

"Well, I stayed with my friend for a few days and then traveled around Switzerland and Austria for a bit.

Oh—while I was still at Sondra's, Nikos called me from Greece a couple of times. Then we met about two weeks ago in Vienna. We, uh, decided to spend the next few days together before coming to Greece, so..."

"So you and Nikos ended up in Vienna together."

Janelle was acutely aware of the not-so-subtle shift in his tone. He had warned her that she would have no secrets from him, personal or otherwise. She lifted her chin and stared at him, refusing to be intimidated. "Yes."

"And this was when you became...intimate with Mr. Marinatos."

It wasn't a question; it was a statement of fact. She wasn't at all sure she liked this line of questioning or this man.

"Yes."

"How did it come about?"

"I beg your pardon?"

He affected deliberate patience. "Did you initiate it or did he?"

Her chin lifted higher. "I don't remember."

"It was only two weeks ago, Miss Lindsey."

Her mouth grew tight. "He initiated it."

"How?"

"How? How do you think!"

"There are lots of ways."

Janelle frowned into Alec's eyes. His rigid seriousness frightened her, making her all the more aware of how desperately frail her situation was. Her freedom was hanging by a tenuous thread. Her life and her short-lived career in foreign service were on the verge of collapse. A man she had known intimately, albeit briefly, was now dead—and she was being charged with his murder!

Why had the embassy sent Alec Hayden? Why hadn't Bluminfeld come himself?

"I really don't remember," she finally said, thinking back to those glorious carriage rides in the streets of Vienna, listening to Strauss waltzes in the parks, drinking *einspanner* and eating apple strudel in the cafés. She knew, after that one night, that she hadn't been in love with Nikos. It had only been the city, the music, the wine, the first taste of freedom. Going to bed with him had been a mistake. But she hadn't made many mistakes in her life. Other people made lots of them. Couldn't she be forgiven for this one?

She swallowed the pain and wrapped her fingers around the glass in front of her. "One thing just led to another. I told you before, he was very charming."

"Obviously."

She looked back at him, her eyes snapping with hot lights. "Is this really necessary?"

"Yes."

"For whom? You or the investigation?"

His insensitive gaze swept over her. Her face was angular, but the smoky brown eyes and full lips softened the determined lines. From what he could see of her body, there were no sharp angles. Only soft curves. His eyes centered steellike on her face. "I personally could not care less what you do with your body, Miss Lindsey. I don't even want to be here right now. I was scheduled to go to Turkey this afternoon. I could have been relaxing on a Mediterranean beach tomorrow morning if you hadn't gotten yourself arrested."

"Gotten myself arrested?" she snapped. "I didn't get myself arrested, Mr. Hayden. I *was* arrested. And I am being falsely accused of a crime I did not com-

mit. I am an American citizen, on the embassy staff. I
deserve better than this.''

"You deserve better only if you are innocent.''

"I am innocent!'' she yelled, and the sound of her
cry echoed along the thick brick walls of the police
station, causing every head in the room to turn toward her.

Alec leaned back in his chair and slowly drank his
water while never taking his eyes off her. The long
braid had swung forward, falling over her left shoulder. Her eyes were like two live coals, burning bright
in a face whose expression was full of righteous indignation. He wasn't sure what to make of her. Aside
from the fact that she was the daughter of the late
Thomas Lindsey, a highly respected dignitary, she was
interesting in a lot of other ways. Her file spelled innocence with a capital *I*. But he had lived in a world
of gray ambiguities and mistrust for so long, he had
lost the ability to see the naive and candid side of life.
In Alec's line of work, no one ever told the truth about
anything. So whether she was guilty or innocent in this
case, he was as yet undecided. The jury was still out.

Something Hayden had said earlier jogged Janelle's memory, and her voice dwindled away to a tired
whisper as she said, "Nikos was really a thief?''

"Yes.''

"I didn't know.'' She stared down at her clenched
hands. "What is going to happen to me?''

Alec hesitated, but only for a second. "You have to
stay in jail . . . for tonight.''

She swallowed the lump of fear that was jammed
into the back of her throat. "Is it . . . safe?''

"You're . . . with the embassy,'' he said, but she noticed that he hesitated a little too much between words

and that he loosened his tie even more, as if it were still choking him. "You work for Bluminfeld. He'll make sure you are taken care of. You'll be safe."

She wasn't going to panic. She wasn't going to cry. Not in front of Alec Hayden. She'd wait until she was alone. She cleared her throat to force the tears down. "And . . . tomorrow? What will happen then?"

His eyes were locked with hers. He saw the tears, but he wouldn't let them faze him. She had been connected with Nikos Marinatos. And Marinatos had been killed before Alec could get the information he was after. That information was his primary concern right now. Of course, it was always possible that Janelle Lindsey could be of more use to him out of jail than in. But he would have to think about that later.

He forced himself to look away from her bewildered face and spoke in a clipped voice. "Tomorrow, we'll talk some more."

Chapter Three

The sign on the door read Minister of Antiquities and Restoration, and the man behind the antique desk was a perfect fit for the role. The top of his head was balding, and the thin gray hair at the sides was swept back behind his ears. His dark suit coat was frayed; his tie was a previous decade too wide. The office that surrounded him was piled knee-high with fossilized clutter. Beneath bushy brows, Vasilos Voutsas regarded Alec with guarded respect.

"This person you refer to..."

"Mavro Sklavopoulos," Alec repeated.

"Yes, my assistant. I am afraid I do not understand, Mr. Hayden. You say you received some sort of—how do you say?—anonymous call. About Mavro?"

"Yes. According to the anonymous source in your office, Mavro Sklavopoulos and a man named Nikos Marinatos were involved in something illegal."

"This Nikos Marinatos...he is the man you say was murdered this morning?"

"Yes."

"Since when, Mr. Hayden, did the American government start concerning itself with illegal matters in my country?"

"The American Department of State was contacted by someone in your ministry who obviously felt that our government should be made aware of this situation."

"But what situation, I ask you? And why did this—this anonymous person not tell me? I am the Greek minister of antiquities."

Alec leaned back in his chair. "I have been asking myself the same question, Mr. Voutsas."

The minister scowled across the space of his desk. "If the Americans feel that they have some concern in—in whatever these—how do you say?—alleged activities are, then why is it that this person did not simply call the American embassy here in Athens?"

Alec crossed one ankle over his knee and affected a casual, mildly interested pose. He was glad he had decided not to speak Greek with the minister. The subtleties that he wanted to convey were easier to express in English. "That question, Minister Voutsas, is still under investigation."

"I see," said the minister, regarding Alec with a dark, penetrating stare. "Am I to understand that an American or Americans are involved with my assistant and this—the dead man? Perhaps," he added coolly, his heavy brows arched, "someone in your embassy in my city?"

"I have implied no such thing," Alec answered. "And—" he paused for effect "—I am sure that the distinguished minister of antiquities and restoration is not suggesting that anyone with the American embassy is involved in anything illegal."

The distinguished minister of antiquities and restoration did not answer. He was watching Alec Hayden with the same intensity that was being directed toward him. He had been with the department for too many years to discount the possibility that one of his employees might be involved in illegal activities. God knew, the temptation for extra money was always present in government work. And while Americans seemed to find it difficult to understand, bribery in the everyday work world of Greece was an accepted practice. But this young man from the United States government seemed to be inferring something more than a small, harmless bribe. Somehow there was a connection between Mavro and the American embassy and a dead man. Yet if there was something sour in one of his departments, he—Vasilos Voutsas—would discover it.

In less than ten years he would be allowed to retire from government service. His wife had died three years ago, but when he retired, he would take her mother and father and brothers and all of the children to his small farm in Epirus, where the gray rocks flamed with deep pinks and violets and where the mountains were heroic and stalwart. He would make sure that he left his office with honor, without a hint of scandal attached to his name. From what little this Mr. Hayden had sketched out, it seemed that he, Vasilos Voutsas, would have to find Mavro Sklavopoulos and get to the bottom of the matter.

"You say Sklavopoulos is on holiday?" Alec asked.

"Yes. He is not expected to return for two more weeks. You understand, yes?"

"Of course, but can you contact him?"

"I fear he is…oh, your language is very difficult for me."

"Out of touch?"

Vasilos Voutsas stared at Alec. "I am afraid I do not know this phrase…'out of touch.' But the truth is that I do not know where he went. I will try to locate him."

"If you do find him, I'd like to talk to him."

"Certainly."

Alec smiled and glanced about the cluttered office. "Have any major antiquities disappeared in the past few months?"

Major antiquities? Voutsas asked himself, wondering what the American might consider major. And was that what this was all about? Perhaps some professor from the United States was claiming that his dig site had been robbed. But surely the Department of State would not concern itself with something like that.

"Items disappear all the time," Voutsas answered. "It is impossible to stop the flow of illegal trafficking. We try, but it is a frustrating task. Archaeological digs are ongoing. You Americans carry out most of the important studies. Items of importance are stolen all the time—prehistoric, medieval, pre-Hellenic. I have even had numerous reports over the past couple of years of Byzantine relics that have been stolen from Orthodox churches and shrines." He lifted his hands in a gesture of helplessness. "So you see, Mr. Hayden, it does not end."

"Have you ever heard the name Boris Ivanov?"

The minister kept his face perfectly blank. He, too, could play ignorant when he thought it might help. He wanted to hear what this Mr. Alec Hayden knew. That was the way to learn. He shrugged. "No, I believe not."

"Mavro never mentioned that name to you?"

"No. Ivanov. . ." he mused. "Is that Russian?"

"Yes."

"You seem to know much that you are not telling me, Mr Hayden."

"No, I'm just looking for answers. And I have lots of questions."

The minister smiled thinly. "You, of course, will share these answers with me when you learn them."

"Of course. And you will do the same for me."

"But certainly."

The two men smiled warily at each other.

"But I must tell you, Mr. Hayden," said Vasilos Voutsas, "that I have been known to be a suspicious man."

Alec stood up and held out his hand to the government official. "Good. Then we will be seeing much more of each other."

"I am certain that we will."

THE DARKNESS SWEPT OVER Janelle, clinging to her, covering her completely. She sat alone on the cot, her shoulders slumped as she stared vacantly into the silent black void.

Nothing in her life had prepared her for this. In fact, now that she thought about it, she realized she had been prepared for one thing and one thing only—a life in the diplomatic corps. No other options had ever been presented or pursued.

It had been easy, in some ways, not having to worry about what the future would hold. All she had had to do was study hard, follow the set guidelines for behavior, learn as many languages as she could and, in general, be a perfect individual. That wasn't so tough, was it?

Janelle sighed and closed her eyes, but the inner darkness was equally overwhelming. Nothing she had ever done had been quite right. She had tried so hard to please her parents, wanting so badly to gain their approval. She had followed them from pillar to post with never a complaint. She had learned the duties of an ambassador's daughter and had practiced them diligently. Even when her few friends had tempted her with their youthful rebellion and reckless fun, she had not varied from the path her parents had expected her to follow.

Sometimes, she wished she had. It was as if she was unprepared for life outside the embassy. Within its walls, she could function without a flaw or a moment of uncertainty. But outside, in the real world, she was at a loss.

The relationship with Nikos had been the first she'd had in years. At home, she'd been too well guarded ever to attract the boys in her school. In college, she'd always been too busy studying. On vacation breaks, her parents had expected her home to help them entertain. There had never been time to develop romantic relationships with anyone her own age. Besides, all her male peers had always seemed so immature. She had spent her youth around adults. She had never known how to be young.

Nikos had brought out her latent passion. His dark eyes and overt sexuality had been a tantalizing attraction, hinting at a wild side in her that she couldn't resist. He was everything she was supposed to avoid, everything she had been sheltered from by her parents. But her parents were gone now. Her father had died two years ago of a heart attack, and her mother had recently remarried and was living in California. No one was around to tell Janelle no. And so, for the first time in her life, she had let nature dictate her actions.

It had turned out to be the worst mistake of her life.

She had known that right after they'd made love. Almost overnight, Nikos had become brutally possessive. But his attentiveness had nothing to do with any great love that he felt for her. Instead, he had constantly prodded her for information about the embassy and her job there. It didn't take her long to realize that he had been after something more than her heart and body from the first. He was not the same man she had been with in Vienna. His sudden bouts of anger frightened her, since she didn't know how to deal with them. She could not ignore the possibility that his anger might erupt into an act of violence against her. In her limited experience, no man like Nikos had ever come along. She'd felt utterly defenseless against him.

And now Nikos was dead, and she was being charged with his murder. Had he actually been a thief?

A new series of chills raced along her spine, and the taste of fear was bitter in the back of her mouth. What was she going to do? Her parents had always taken care of her, whisking away any threat of danger or trouble. But now she had no one.

No one, except for Alec Hayden. He was the only person who had been sent to help her—who *could* help her. The trouble was, he didn't believe her. He had disapproved of her relationship with Nikos. That much was obvious. No doubt he thought of her as some kind of airhead who flitted from one man's bed to another. Those gray, disapproving eyes of his saw what they wanted to see. And that was what scared Janelle the most now. Because if he didn't believe her, if he didn't help her, she was lost. She had no one else to turn to.

The long dark hours dragged around her, pulling her deeper and deeper into herself. She cried tears for Nikos, and for her father, and for herself. Especially for herself. But in the end, the tears changed nothing. Her fate still hinged on the belief of one man.

"I BELIEVE HER."

"Have a cigar." James Eddington Bluminfeld held the open box across the desk for Alec.

Hayden shook his head. "Thanks, no."

The chargé carefully closed the box and set it down, making sure it was lined up perfectly with the edge of the desk. He laid his palms face down in front of him on the rosewood surface, as if reassuring himself that the office and the new job were really his. "Perhaps your judgment is faulty."

"I don't think so."

Bluminfeld's tapered fingernails began to drum on the desk. "What makes you so sure?"

"I presumed guilt all along with her, from the beginning. She didn't back down."

"So she's a good poker player."

Hayden shook his head again. "I don't buy it. Either she's an amazingly qualified actress or she's telling the simple truth. I believe she's telling the truth."

Bluminfeld opened his drawer and extracted three bottles of pills. He opened the first and poured two red capsules into his palm, tossed them to the back of his mouth, then washed them down with a glass of water. Two white tablets followed. The third bottle went back into the drawer, unopened.

The embassy was quiet at this time of night. The echoing footsteps of the guards outside the office door were the only sounds they heard. Bluminfeld cleared his throat. "I expected something different from you, Alec. You have a reputation, of sorts. I didn't expect you to be completely bowled over by those big brown eyes of hers."

"I stayed to deal with the authorities because of who she is. I'm not here to help them crucify her."

Bluminfeld's hands were once again flattened on the desk. He stared at Alec, weighing the man's power. Hayden did carry a lot of clout in the State Department. He could cause trouble. Still, the situation with Janelle Lindsey had to be wrapped up...clean.

"The man was murdered in her house," Bluminfeld ventured. "And the police have a note that links her to him in something more than a personal relationship. She is to give something to this—this Zafer person. The police know Nikos was a thief. So obviously Janelle is involved in something, well, a bit unsavory, to say the least."

Alec had thought about that note quite a bit. He had finally decided that Janelle Lindsey would be a much bigger help to him out of jail. He shrugged off Bluminfeld's remark. "Circumstantial evidence. It won't hold up in court."

"We're in Greece, Alec. The American judicial system doesn't apply."

Alec leaned forward in his chair and rested a forearm on the desk. "I've spent the better part of my adult life in international law, Bluminfeld. I'll fight it." He sat back. "You know I can."

Yes, the chargé knew that Alec Hayden could do that. He could stir up plenty of trouble . . . for everyone. Bluminfeld stared at the spot where Hayden's forearm had rested. He took a soft polishing cloth from the drawer and carefully restored the gleam to the dark wood. "The police are going to want to continue investigating this."

Alec nodded. "I know that. But she doesn't have to be detained while they investigate."

Bluminfeld sat quietly, thinking about it. "We would have to give them our assurance that she wouldn't leave the city."

"I think they would accept that."

"Well, what if she were to bolt? Imagine what that would do to our credibility!"

"If she knew the consequences . . ."

"Consequences!" Bluminfeld sneered. "A fairly shallow word considering the circumstances."

"You're assuming she's guilty."

Bluminfeld fell back into the folds of his leather chair and pressed his fingers into his temples. "Oh, I just don't know. I'm not saying the girl is guilty. It's only that—well, I'm going to have to think about this."

Alec leaned forward again and dropped his forearms onto the spot the chargé had just polished. His voice was low and carefully paced with the intimidating confidence that had been developed early in his law career. It had also proved to be a useful asset in cutting through the haze of political nondialogue that constituted the bureaucratic mumble. "I'm going back to the police station in the morning, James. And to-

morrow afternoon I'll be on a plane to Ankara. I never
leave loose ends."

Bluminfeld had known from the beginning of this
incident how it would be with Hayden. He didn't just
check out a situation, he dove headfirst into it and
swam around, moving pieces here and there until
everything fitted exactly the way he wanted it to. Of
course, there wasn't much point in worrying about it.
The damage was already done.

"I understand," the chargé said finally. "I'll take
care of her release."

Alec leaned back in his chair and smiled. "Good.
Now, how about one of those cigars?"

NARROW WINDING STREETS intersected and spiraled
like worms wriggling in a jar. Dark walkways bright-
ened by boisterous tavernas were sliced by stairs leading up to color-washed houses with clay-tiled roofs.
The two men stood in an alley next to a broken and
chipped stairway that plunged down into an un-
lighted cellar filled with wine vats. One of the men
struck a match on the stucco wall and cupped his hand
over the tip of his cigarette until the flame caught. He
took several deep drags, filling the air with the strong
smell of Turkish tobacco. He waited for the American to speak.

"There is a slight...change." The American
expected some response to his words, but the other
man continued to smoke in silence. "As of tomorrow, the subject will no longer be detained, so different arrangements will have to be made."

"I see," the man said, his voice low and guttural.

"You will take care of those arrangements, Boris?"

Boris Ivanov took another drag on his cigarette and glanced down the alleyway, verifying the shadows that flickered with each swing of the hanging lamps from the tavernas. "I always do," he said. "The coin...has she admitted to having it?"

The American shook his head. "Not yet. But she will."

"You seem very sure of yourself."

"One way or another, she will give it to us. I expect payment as soon as the shipment is made."

Boris dropped the cigarette and ground it out beneath his heel. "Then we must get it from her. I will not be patient for long. The matter must be taken care of soon." That said, he turned and walked down the dark alley to disappear beyond the curve that delved into the ancient Plaka quarter.

The American watched him go, then turned and walked in the opposite direction, toward the government limousine that was parked around the corner. But what he wished he could do was head for the bright lights and music of the nearest taverna.

THE BLACK LIMOUSINE pulled up and parked in full sunlight before Janelle's brick town house. Professor Goulandris's home was a holdout from another age. It crouched between new high-rise flats that had sprung up where old homes of well-to-do families used to be. Progress and cement mixers had metamorphosed Athens into a city with a very ancient past and an almost choking present, but with almost nothing left standing of the eighteen centuries in between.

The driver held the door for Alec and Janelle. They stepped out and stood on the sidewalk before the tall iron gate. Janelle took a deep breath and relished the

sweet taste of freedom for the first time since noon
yesterday. April was the best time in Greece, or so
everyone had told her. Warm and balmy, the country
was not yet stifled by the heat of summer and the
constant noise of tourists. To the Orthodox faith,
Easter was the most important day of the year, and
from the beginning of April until the middle of May,
villages all over the islands commemorated the holiday with processions, feasts, days of mourning and
days of rejoicing. April was a time of celebration.

"This is a nice neighborhood," Alec noted.

"Yes," she agreed with a smile, glancing up through
the silvery leaves of the olive trees. Even the smog and
the smell of sulfur could not dampen her spirits. Even
if her freedom was only temporary and with restrictions, still she was free. And for now, that was enough.
"They've left much of the native foliage in this
neighborhood, which I understand is a rarity in Athens. I love all those overgrown shrubs at the base of
the house, and the patio in the back is covered by a
latticework of vines that are just beginning to sprout."
She turned toward Alec. "I want to thank you, Mr.
Hayden, for interceding on my behalf and for getting
me released."

"You do understand the restrictions."

"Yes. My prison walls have just grown to encom-
pass the city. But still . . . that is something."

The gate squeaked when he swung it open. "You
cannot leave until the investigation is complete."

Janelle walked past him and up the sidewalk. He
followed one step behind her. "How long will that
take?"

"Until they find the murderer."

She stopped on the front porch and looked at him. "Yesterday they thought they had their murderer."

"That was yesterday."

She held the key to the door in her hand, but she continued to look at Alec, her head cocked. He wore jeans, and an oxford cloth shirt, and a navy sport coat. The red tie obviously had been an afterthought. The few gray streaks in his hair looked almost blond in the sunlight, and when he took off the dark sunglasses, his eyes crinkled at the corners, making him appear more vulnerable, more human. He was a very handsome man, a fact that had been lost on her in yesterday's emotional turmoil. Then, she had seen only the seriousness, only the cold gray eyes staring down at her. But today he seemed different, younger somehow and more relaxed. "What happened?"

"They decided to investigate further."

"I see. How did you convince them to do that?"

"I have no authority here," he answered. "Bluminfeld handled it."

She slipped the key into the lock and twisted it until it clicked. But she hesitated before turning the knob. "This is—is very difficult."

"Facing the house?"

She kept her eyes on the door. "Yes. It will never be the same, you know."

Alec gently drew her hand away from the knob and replaced it with his own. "You have to go in sometime. Come on, it'll be okay." He pushed the door open and, with his hand on her elbow, propelled her into the foyer.

She had been prepared, as much as one could be, for a kind of eerie chill. No one could simply walk into a house in which someone had been brutally murdered and remain totally unaffected. But she had not been prepared for the nightmarish scene that now confronted her. She didn't even recognize the house.

The wide doorway that led into the *salotto*—a kind of informal living room—framed the chaos. Furniture had been knocked over, books lay in jumbled piles on the floor, the cushions from the couch had been tossed to the floor and slashed, and their stuffing trailed in dusty white piles across everything. A lamp was overturned in the center of the room, surrounded by shards of glass from the bulb.

Her heart began pounding loudly in her chest and throat, and she had to forcefully fight back the nausea. "What..." She could not continue. Her throat was suddenly too dry and constricted. She glanced at Alec, whose expression was blank. She reached for the doorcase to support herself, but it was Alec's arm that she clutched. He led her into the room and, after replacing the cushion on the big wing chair, guided her into the seat.

Janelle pressed a hand across her mouth, as if that gesture could stem the tears in her eyes. "What has happened?" she whispered. "Why... what..." She shook her head. "I don't understand."

"It's okay," he said, brushing some loose strands of hair back from her face. "It can be straightened up."

She regarded him with dismay. "How can this possibly be straightened up? Surely—surely the police didn't do this!"

He surveyed the room and then looked back at her. "They searched the house thoroughly, but no, I don't think they did this."

"Then who?" she cried, not even bothering now to hide the tears. "Who could have done this?"

He shook his head slowly. "I don't know." He moved away from her and picked up the lamp lying on the floor. After he'd set it back on the end table, he began to replace the couch cushions, turning the slashed sides facedown. "Do you have a broom or a vacuum cleaner?"

She looked at him as if she had never heard of either. "How—how will I explain this to the owner of the house? This furniture...it's all his."

Alec walked over to the row of shelves and stooped down to gather the books. "It's on loan to the embassy?"

She had lost track of the conversation. "What?"

"This house—is it loaned to the embassy?"

"Oh...yes. I..." The thought trailed away as she stared at a tuft of batting from the couch that lay in a pile on the carpet.

"Then Bluminfeld will take care of it," Alec was saying. "You don't need to worry about it."

"Yes," she replied in a monotone.

He picked up several handfuls of books and lined them up on the shelf. When he had finished, he turned back to Janelle. She was sitting so still, staring at the carpet. "Do you have any liquor in the house? Any liquor?" he repeated.

She looked up. "Hmm? Oh, no, I'm sorry. I—I have some tea in the kitchen if you want it."

"I don't want it for me," he said. "Where's the kitchen?"

She waved her hand in a vague gesture and then went back to staring at the floor. Alec left the room in search of the kitchen. He found it and began opening cabinets, although most of the contents had been strewn about on the counters. The tea bags were in the cabinet next to the sink. After filling a pan with some bottled water from the refrigerator, he put the pan on the stove to heat. He moved around the kitchen distractedly, thinking about the woman in the other room. It hadn't been easy getting her released, and he owed a hell of a lot of favors now. But he had decided that she was of no use to him in jail. He just hoped he had made the right decision. With her emotional state as fragile as it was, he wasn't so sure.

The water was boiling, so he picked up the pan and poured the liquid into a cup. He dropped in the bag of tea, let it steep, then carried the cup out to Janelle. She looked more alert now, he noticed as he placed the hot drink in her hands.

"Feeling better?" he asked.

"Yes, much, thanks." Janelle sipped gratefully at the tea. "Thank you for straightening up this mess. I shudder to think what the rest of the house looks like."

"The kitchen wasn't too bad. Listen, I'll call the embassy from the airport, and they can send someone over to clean."

She glanced up, startled. "Airport?" Her only ally was leaving already?

"I have to go to Turkey. Just for one day."

"And then you'll—you'll come back here?"

"Yes."

Her sigh was audible. She hated to feel so dependent on anyone. But right now, he was the only friend she had. She wasn't sure what everyone at the embassy thought about her. Alec had already said that Bluminfeld wouldn't let her come back to work until this business was cleared up. Maybe the entire staff believed that she was guilty.

The hot tea felt good sliding down her throat. She smiled at him. "What are you here for, Mr. Hayden?"

"What do you mean?" His response was curt and almost rude, but she let it pass.

"I mean, what do you do for the State Department?"

"Oh," he said, his tone more level. "Well, lots of things, really. Right now I'm checking up on security at all the embassies."

"A rather pressing need in this day and age. Working in the foreign service is certainly not what it used to be."

"Being an American is not what it used to be."

Janelle saw him glance at his watch. "Listen, I know you have to go. Don't stay on my account." She had meant to sound practical and independent. She had not meant to cry. But that was exactly what she was doing.

Alec reached for the cup that was teetering in her hands and set it on the floor. "It's okay," he murmured, feeling all at once inept and clumsy. He wasn't used to women like this, women with honest emotions. He wasn't sure how he was supposed to react.

"I'm sorry," she sobbed, cupping her hands over her eyes. She started to lean too far forward, so he wrapped his arms awkwardly around her and patted her back.

"Shh, Miss Lindsey. It's going to be all right. Please don't cry." He stroked the back of her hair. She felt soft in his arms, defenseless, as if in that moment she needed his care and protection above and beyond all else. He abruptly set her back in the chair and stood up. Caring for a woman who was an emotional wreck was not part of the deal. He pulled a handkerchief from his pocket and handed it over.

"Thank you," she whispered, dabbing at her eyes. "I . . . I don't know what made me . . ." Oh, don't be ridiculous, Janelle, she scolded herself. Of course you know what made you do that. In the past twenty-four hours, you've found a dead body on your floor, been arrested and locked away in a dark cell, been interrogated by a man from the State Department and found your house in utter shambles. You don't owe anyone any apologies.

She looked up at Alec. He was shifting uncomfortably in front of her, his expression for the first time revealing less than total confidence. "I'm fine now," she said.

He stood there as if he were waiting for her to crumble again.

"Really," she insisted. "I will be all right now. You'd better go so you can catch your plane."

He let out a slow breath, still hesitating. "If you're sure."

She gave him back his handkerchief, and he crammed it into his back pocket. "Yes, quite." Oh, God, why didn't he just leave! She wanted him out of there before she broke down again. She was scared to death to be alone, but she was even more afraid to ask him to stay.

At the short, shrill ring of the telephone, they both jumped. Alec stared at the instrument on the end table with the same suspicious, disapproving glare he had directed toward Janelle in the police station. He glanced back at her, but she only shrugged. "It's nothing," she said. "No one knows this number. Only the embassy has it."

"What if it's someone from the embassy?"

"No, we have a sort of code. They ring once and hang up, and then I call back. I told you, it's essential that we keep a low profile."

The phone rang several more times before it finally stopped. Janelle walked Alec to the front door, opened it, and saw the limousine still parked outside, waiting to take him to the airport. He was an important man, with important things to do and places to go. She was a frightened woman who, as he had said yesterday, had gotten herself arrested. It was her problem. She would have to handle it on her own.

She held out her hand to him. He was very serious and controlled, almost aloof, but also very handsome. It would have been nice to have met him under different circumstances. "I really do want to thank you for all you've done."

He took her hand. "Just doing my job."

"Yes, I know," she said, pulling her hand back reluctantly. "But tell me something, Mr. Hayden. Do you think I'm guilty?"

His gaze remained squarely on her eyes. "I deal only in the truth, Miss Lindsey. That's all I ever look at."

"And what is the truth?"

The phone began to ring again, and he glanced through the open front door.

"I told you," she said. "It's nothing. I get wrong numbers all the time. The telephone system in Greece is not on a par with AT&T. But you didn't answer my question, Mr. Hayden, about what is the truth."

He hesitated until the phone stopped, then slipped on his dark sunglasses. "The truth is that I have to go."

Her mouth tightened, and she took a step backward into the foyer. "Well, thank you again."

"You're sure you're all right now?"

"Yes, perfectly sure." She smiled with false brightness. "The worst is over. What could possibly happen to me now?"

At that moment, the telephone decided to ring for the third time. Alec stared at Janelle, then turned abruptly and walked down the sidewalk, through the iron gate and into the waiting black limousine.

She closed the door and leaned her back against it. Her head was throbbing painfully. And why didn't that damn phone stop ringing?

After what seemed like an eternity, she could take the sound of it no longer. She strode through the foyer and snatched up the living room phone. There was silence after her "hello", only the hiss of airwaves carried through the wires. She started to hang up, but the silence suddenly took shape and congealed into a menacing voice.

"Janelle Lindsey?"

Ice-cold fingers of fear slid up her spine. "Yes?"

The low, guttural voice came clearly through the wire. "My name is Boris. Remember that name, Miss Lindsey, because soon we will meet. You have twenty-four hours. Twenty-four hours to turn over the coin. Twenty-four hours to live."

Chapter Four

The phone slipped from Janelle's icy fingers. A draft of air circled over her, but when she stumbled back into the foyer, she saw that the door was closed. It had simply been her imagination. Maybe, just maybe, the voice on the other end of the line had been her imagination, also. No. She had heard the sounds distinctly enough. The words were frozen on her mind like a thin glaze of rime on a winter field.

She yanked open the door and stared at the patch of sunlight on which the limousine had been parked. Alex Hayden was gone. She closed the door slowly. She was on her own.

She walked into the living room, moving like a zombie, and dropped into the wing chair. She was aware of nothing but a raw chill that clamped around her bones, strangling her. She didn't want to move, didn't even want to think. She wanted the cold to wrap itself around her and anesthetize all the pain in her body. But the thoughts kept coming, unbidden, unwelcome. She didn't want them, but they persisted. So she knew she had to force herself to think rationally. She was not going to panic. There was a logical explanation for this, as there was for everything else in life. She would simply have to sit quietly and let it come.

The afternoon shadows slid silently across the room, skirting the edge of the huge dark credenza that stretched along the far wall. Loukas Goulandris had an eclectic sense of style when it came to his home. Nothing matched, yet somehow everything blended into a thoroughly Greek statement. But someone had made a statement of his own yesterday, and neither the room nor the furnishings would ever be the same again.

She had to think. It would all make sense if she could just piece everything together the right way. Nikos dead—murdered in her bedroom. The police had found a note that he had apparently written to her. *Don't give it up to anyone but Zafer.* It...it...it. She had spent the night in jail, and then this morning she had quite surprisingly been released. The investigation would continue...the note...what had Nikos meant to tell her in that note...? It...the man on the phone, Boris, *remember that name*...twenty-four hours to give him the coin...what coin...? Was that the "it" Nikos had spoken of in the note...? And Zafer, where did he fit into all of this...?

Janelle felt a wave of fatigue rush over her, dragging and twisting and pulling her in all directions. But her mind would not let her rest. Where *did* Zafer fit in?

She had met him when she and Nikos first arrived in Athens. He had been at the station to meet their train and was introduced as a longtime friend of the Marinatos family. Janelle had immediately liked him. Zafer had that special quality of open-arm Greek hospitality that kept foreigners slightly off balance.

Full of the innocence and curiosity that typified so many of his countrymen, he'd stared at her with his dark eyes and proceeded to ask her the most personal of questions. Never imagining that he might be probing into areas where questions were simply not welcome, he had smiled patiently and waited for her answers.

But the note... Nikos had told her to give it—whatever *it* was—to Zafer. Yes, that would make sense. If Nikos were in some kind of trouble, who better to turn to than his trusted friend?

Janelle knew, too, that she could trust him. She would have to. There was no one else.

The telephone on the table next to her emitted a short ring and then was silent. She stared at the black instrument, afraid to breathe, afraid to touch it. One short ring. Her breath came out slowly. The caller would be someone from the embassy.

She picked up the receiver and dialed the number. After Janelle identified herself, the switchboard operator immediately transferred her to Frank Osborn's office.

"Howdy, Janelle."

"Hello, Mr. Osborn."

"I just wanted to give you a ring to see how you're doing. We're all a mite worried about you over here."

"Thank you. I really appreciate that. I...as a matter of fact, Mr. Osborn, something has just happened that I think you should know about."

"Oh?"

"Yes. I—I received a phone call earlier. I wasn't going to answer it, but the caller was so insistent. The phone just kept ringing and ringing."

"And?"

"Well, he threatened me and . . ."

"Who did?"

"He said his name was Boris."

Dead silence met her from the other end of the line.

"Mr. Osborn?"

"Yes, I'm here. This Boris—what did he say?"

"That I have twenty-four hours to give him the coin."

"You're sure he said his name was Boris?"

"Positive."

"And you, uh, you have this coin?"

"No. That's the thing. I have no idea what he was talking about. I'm really scared, Mr. Osborn. I don't know what to do."

"Now, you just hold on there," he said smoothly. "It was probably a crank caller."

Janelle frowned. Surely the chief of security didn't believe that. "He said my name. He knew who I was. This was no crank call."

"Have you been in contact with anyone else? Does Alec Hayden know about this?"

"No, but . . ."

"But what?"

"Well, Nikos had a friend named Zafer. He was the one who was mentioned in that note the police have. I—I think I'm going to talk with him. Maybe he can give me some answers."

There was a long span of silence from the other end. "You're going to meet this Zafer fella in Athens?"

"Of course. I'm not supposed to leave the city, remember? I haven't called him yet, so I don't know if he will meet with me at all, but I have to try something. Don't you agree?"

"As head of security, I don't think I can rightfully tell you what you should do, except...be careful. You never know in this town when someone is going to come up right behind you. You have a good day, now, Janelle."

She fought down the panic. "Yes. Goodbye, Mr. Osborn."

With a strange look on her face, she slowly replaced the receiver. She felt the hair at the back of her neck stand on end, as if someone were indeed right behind her, breathing on her. She spun around in her chair and gasped, but there was nothing there. Only a skittering shadow fell across the wall. Yet for the first time in her life, Janelle Lindsey could not categorically discount the existence of ghosts.

THE FIVE MEN sat on crates in the abandoned building. The electricity did not work, but one of the men had thought to bring a coal lantern with him. It was the only light in the room. Outside in the darkened street, all was quiet.

A large man with graying hair and sharp, thin features began to pace the floor, speaking gruffly in Russian to one of the men. "Have all the items left the docks, Sergei?"

"We have a shipment waiting at the train station, sir. Once we have the chalice, we will send everything."

"Good. Make sure nothing goes wrong."

"But, Boris," another man asked, "what about our American friend? Won't he be expecting his prize?"

"The girl has it," Boris growled. "And I expect to get it from her before Zafer Demir does."

"I can take care of Demir," Sergei stated with confidence.

"No," Boris snapped, this time in English. "I want Mavro to do it." He looked at the morose man who was now wringing his hands in front of him. "You understand what I want?"

The Greek began to sweat. "You cannot possibly mean . . . I wanted no part of . . ." The words fell away under Boris's hard glare. Mavro wrung his hands again. "Yes, whatever you wish."

Boris smiled. "Good. Now, as we all know, Demir is in the habit of moving around. I believe he is in Athens now, but he may not remain here for long. You must take care of him immediately."

"And if I, uh, can't find him?"

"You will find him, Mavro. Do not come back to me until the job is done."

"And the girl?" Sergei asked.

Boris stared over the heads of the four men, looking at something beyond the wall, beyond their limited realm of vision. "The girl, yes," he murmured distractedly. "She is nothing, really. A slight annoyance. I will take care of her."

ALEC SHIFTED on the bed and threw one bare leg over the top of the sheet. His sleep had been erratic, filled with the discordant sounds of the Ankara street below his window.

But from somewhere deep within himself, he could hear the clack of a train and sense the wheels turning, clicking: he could feel the rhythmic rocking of the car and the body in his arms, Erin's body, her skin slick and moist, her blond hair streaming around her face. He was holding her, and he was also standing across the compartment, watching someone else hold her, and they were laughing at him. Then he was in a desert, and three Greek policemen were holding a woman, a different woman with dark hair and brown eyes, and he wondered where Erin was. A caravan of Arabs leading camels passed by, and he and the dark-haired woman were thirsty, but no one would give them water. And then he was alone in the dark, and only a thin shaft of light shone on the woman from across the room. She lifted her hands to her hair and smiled, and he could feel the smile wash over him as her braid slowly came down. And then he was on the train again, but this time he was moving fast down the corridors, running, searching for someone's compartment. He opened doors, but in each compartment Erin was with a different man, and he slammed the doors and the train whistle blew.

Alec opened his eyes and lay very still, listening to sounds of the city. Even through the closed window of the hotel room, he could hear the blare of horns and the rumble of trucks along the street. But he welcomed the noise. He welcomed anything that would pull the disturbing dream away from him.

He glanced over at the other side of the bed. It was empty. He was alone. But that was okay. Except for the occasional nights when he was lucky enough to have a soft, warm body to hold, he had been alone for a long time. Somehow, it no longer mattered.

His marriage to Erin had cured him of the need for permanence. With her, he had been cured of a lot of things. Things like trust, devotion, undying love. Those qualities and emotions he had gladly relinquished to the rest of the world's suckers. He was free of them—forever.

The job didn't allow much time for personal fulfillment anyway. And that had most likely been the instigator of all the problems in his marriage. Erin had seemed to think so. There had never been enough time to build relationships with anybody. When he had worked for the Bureau in Atlanta years ago, the patterns had been set. Career was everything. And, in truth, that was probably why he had progressed as far as he had. He had left the Bureau at twenty-nine and spent the past eight years charging up the ladder at the State Department. An up-and-comer, he had been called at twenty-nine. Now he was called simply an expert.

He glanced over at the window. Only a sliver of light edged through the slit in the curtains, even though the moon was full. The smog from the coal furnaces and factories blanketed the city in a gray shroud. *Expert.* He wished he knew what the hell that was supposed to mean.

He knew it meant sitting higher on the pay scale, having an office with a view, picking the assignments he wanted and delegating the rest to those with less clout. But in the long run, what the hell did it really mean? Someday he would be too old for all this running around. Someday he would no doubt be asked to take a teaching position at some quiet but significant New England university. And he would no doubt accept the offer. But would that mean he was exceptionally qualified to mold young minds? Or that he had made a great contribution in the realm of international law and could therefore make an even greater contribution in the world of academia?

He didn't know what the answer was. All he knew was that he would do it alone. Life was remarkably easier that way. He had enough complications in his professional life. He had no need for them in his personal life as well.

He punched and fluffed up the pillow, then clasped his hands behind his head, staring up at the rough textured ceiling. Funny, how one could stay in a Sheraton hotel in any city in the world, and the ceilings were always the same.

He frowned, trying to remember for a minute where he was. Turkey, of course. He had spent the day at the embassy here in Ankara, working for the release of some American businessmen who had been arrested for failing to register their company properly with the Turkish authorities. Tomorrow he would fly back to Athens and see what else he could learn about Nikos Marinatos. He had pulled a lot of strings to get Janelle Lindsey released into his custody. He just hoped she would be of some use to him.

Something flashed across his mind, followed by a burning sensation that gnawed through his lower body. For only a second, he had this bizarre image of her slowly unwinding the dark strands of her hair as she smiled at him from across a room. The purely erotic vision stunned him. He had no idea why it had come into his consciousness.

He tried to ignore the sudden sexual urge that had nudged him, tried to extinguish the curling flame. He needed Janelle Lindsey for one thing only, and that was information. Once he had that, she was on her own.

He reached over for the tape recorder on the table, set it beside him on the bed and flipped on the switch. He listened once again to the sound of her voice. His questions were direct; her answers, for the most part, were solid. Occasionally, there was a lull in the tape before her voice came back, cracked and strained. He listened objectively and closed his eyes. But the image of the dark tresses unwinding and falling into his hands would not go away. She was before him, and suddenly there was no more room for questions and answers, or for thoughts of Ankara or Athens. No more room for disturbing or painful memories of Erin. There was room only for erotic fantasies of the woman he had planned to manipulate. And those sexual images that came from the conscious mind were more disturbing than any feverish dream could ever be.

Chapter Five

Janelle climbed the steep stairs that were cut unevenly into the bare rocks of the hill. White and glaring under the noonday sun, the heat rose in waves to meet the clear blue arch of the sky above. It was a good season on Karpathos, an island between Crete and Rhodes. The stark mountains had turned green again; the Aegean hues were blue and green and crystal clear. The cypress and olive trees sprouted new growth. The fragrance of flowers on the slopes blended with those of the newly blossoming lemon and orange trees. It was a time of renewal. And perched high in the northern mountains, the tiny village of Olimbos—one of the most isolated in all of Greece—was celebrating the renewal of its faith.

It was there that Janelle was to meet Zafer Demir.

The nerves inside her stomach twisted and flexed until they were tied in knots. At every turn she felt as if she were being stalked, as if someone were right behind her. She had not wanted to come. She had told Zafer that she was not allowed to leave Athens. But he had insisted. It was the only way, he had said, that he would meet with her.

Getting to the airport without someone following her had not been easy. Janelle had taken a taxi to the Acropolis and then, from there, had hopped on a bus that carried her to the airport. She had tried to blend in with the crowds of tourists at the foot of the Acropolis, but all she could hope for was that the police were not watching her as closely as they had hinted they would be.

The interisland plane had flown first to Rhodes and then down to the southern end of Karpathos. Upon disembarking, Janelle had had to search for an English-speaking driver willing to take her the remaining twenty-five miles to Olimbos. After haggling over the price and settling finally on one that was far too high, she'd suddenly been besieged by drivers who would be more than delighted to take her wherever she wished to go.

The daredevil she ended up with had driven at breakneck speed along the rough road that wound through the dense forests, climbing ever higher into the forbidding mountains. Until recently there was no road connecting Olimbos to the other eleven villages on the island. She was in luck, or so the driver had informed her with a gleeful smile as he careened around the snaking turns within a hair's width of plummeting off the edge of the cliffs.

On the straightaway, Janelle had relaxed her white knuckles from the edge of the seat and taken in the scenery. Windmills dotted the fields in which women planted new crops. As a major part of the work force on the island, the women of Karpathos wore white Turkish breeches tucked into the tops of long boots, their white skirts looped up and held in place at the waist.

The twenty-five-mile ride had lasted for an hour and a half. Janelle had never been so happy to have her feet planted on terra firma as she was when the driver had deposited her at the base of a long rock stairway that rose to the center of the village. Her only regret was that he would be returning for her at five that afternoon.

From the stone steps, narrow twisting paths led off to humble houses and small, quiet chapels. A priest, wearing a long black robe, pulled a donkey reluctantly down the steep slope beside her. High above, a white bird soared against the azure blue of the sky, then dove for the protective camouflage of the bleached rocks.

An auction was taking place in the village square, so Janelle walked over to a low stone wall and sat down to watch. The villagers shouted out bids for everything from black pottery to honey to sponges the size of basketballs. Basketry and fruit preserves were the first items to be sold. Loaves of bread lined the open market shelves. Dyed eggs of red, yellow and blue were mounded in a pyramid shape between the breads. All around the square were tall clay crocks of freshly made yogurt. In one corner, several large outdoor ovens held roasting lambs and goats for dinner.

The entire village, it seemed, had turned out for this celebration, and Janelle worried if she would ever spot Zafer Demir among the crowd. He had assured her that he would find her, but she began to wonder if that would be possible.

The sun slipped over the midline and started its downhill slide. Janelle watched and waited. But still no Zafer.

At the end of the successful auction, heavy religious icons were loaded onto the men's broad shoulders, and a line of people began to form along the sloping path that led up to the church at the top of the hill. Not knowing what else to do, and unable to keep from being swept along by the pressing tide of participants, Janelle fell into step between a young boy in a red woolen jacket and an old man who clicked his worry beads and groaned painfully as he walked.

Why had Zafer Demir insisted that she meet him in Olimbos? And why had he not shown up? She was taking such a risk in leaving Athens in the first place. If the police found out, she would be thrown straight back in jail. But she had to have answers, and at this point Demir was the only one who could give them to her.

She kept her eyes peeled for him at every turn in the trail. The pathway led along the edge of the cliff, far below which lay the blue Aegean. The procession was helped along by the discordant music of bagpipe, lute, and three-stringed lyre. After a while, Janelle felt a kind of peace well up within her. She turned her face toward the sun and the fresh sea breeze, forgetting for one blissful moment why she was there.

The wet squish of heavy boots beside her and the silhouette that momentarily eclipsed the sun revived the reality.

She stopped in her tracks and swung abruptly toward the man beside her. "Zafer! You're here!"

"Keep walking," he said in a low voice, shifting his head from side to side as he scanned the area with narrowed eyes. "You were followed?"

"No, I—I don't think so."

His expression was grim, his face downcast. This was not the man she remembered, not the happy-go-lucky Greek who had insisted upon toasting her with ouzo when she'd first arrived in his country. But she was not the same as she'd been then, either. Nikos's death had changed everything.

"Why, Zafer? Why did he—was he killed?" Janelle felt the familiar burning behind her eyes, but he did not give her time to cry. He took her arm and spirited her away from the procession, down the path lined with blue-green broom that led back into the center of the village.

She glanced at him while they moved along briskly. His features were as she remembered them—roughly textured skin, black eyebrows that drooped low over dark eyes, a mustache that hung over his thick upper lip. Only the smile that would reveal crooked teeth was missing.

He led her to a corner café whose three lopsided tables and mismatched chairs graced the doorway of a pink stucco house. After she was seated he went inside to order for them both. While he was gone, Janelle tried to formulate the questions she wanted to ask. But she didn't even know where to begin.

The square was almost empty now, except for a few women who had stayed behind to close up the shops and tend to the lambs in the ovens. The wonderful smell filled every nook and cranny of the square, and the happy gossiping voices of the women were carried on the light currents of air.

"This language," Janelle said when Zafer came back and sat down. "I thought I could finally understand a few isolated words in Greek, but I could make out nothing that those people at the auction were saying. And these women . . . it is a different dialect, isn't it?"

He nodded. "That is because this is Karpathos. Here many of our words date back to the time of Homer."

"You are from Olimbos, then?"

"I was born here, yes. My mother, she still lives up at the top of the hill."

"Why did you want me to come here, Zafer? We were both in Athens last night. Why couldn't I speak to you over the phone?"

He propped his arms on the table and stared hard at her, taking in everything in that one piercing glance. "Because there is much to say between you and me, *mou* Jani. No one else must know." He leaned back once again. "You must now tell me everything that has happened to you."

This last statement—although a direct command—was uttered as softly and gently as the breeze that blew down from the mountaintops. Janelle felt all at once cooler and more refreshed than she had felt for several days. She had been right to call him. He would help her solve the puzzle that had broken her life into tiny jagged pieces.

"Well," she began; then her voice wavered with indecision. Now that she had someone to listen to her, someone she could trust, she wasn't even sure what to say. "Nikos di—was murdered. He was..." Her voice dropped to an anguished whisper. "He was murdered in my bedroom." She closed her eyes.

"And then what happened?"

Her eyes flew open. Zafer's mouth was compressed into a tight line, and his voice was strained. But Janelle knew what she was witnessing. It was a classic display of Greek bravado. This man would not dare show grief over his friend in a public café. And never, never in front of a woman.

His stoicism gave her the courage to continue. "And then I was arrested. They accused me of—of the crime." The anguish had returned to her face. "How could they think I could do something like that? He was cold-bloodedly murdered!" A shudder rippled deep inside her body.

Zafer started to speak, but the owner of the tiny café appeared just then with a tin of nectar and a *tirropita* for Janelle and a cup of thick, muddy coffee for Demir. Not until the man had gone back into the house did Zafer speak.

"Last night you said something about a note."

Janelle took a bite of the hot cheese pastry and nodded. "Yes. The police found a note that Nikos had left for me in my house. It said that I must not give it up to anyone but you."

"Yes?"

Janelle stared at the man seated across the table from her. His eyes were burning brightly, and the spark of life had returned to his voice. "I don't know what it is, Zafer. This thing I am supposed to give you—"

"A coin."

She was speechless for several long moments. Finally she was able to find her voice. "That was—that was what the man on the phone said."

Demir's face grew hard. "Man? What man?"

"That was why I wanted to talk to you last night. I wasn't sure how to get in touch with you, but then you called...as if you knew. Just before that a man phoned and told me I must turn over the coin. He—he said I only had twenty-four hours.''

"What did this man sound like? Did he tell you his name?''

"Boris." The intensity of Zafer's dark eyes on her face sent a blaze of fear along her spine. "You—you know the name?''

"Yes. Boris Ivanov.''

"Who is he?''

The intensity vanished from Demir's eyes, and his shrug was philosophical. "The man who threatened you. The man who has threatened me.''

"That's all you know about him?''

"That is all.''

Janelle sighed heavily. She had hoped for so much more. To have an enemy who had no face and no frame of reference in which to place him was more frightening than to confront an enemy head on. "The thing is," she said, frowning, "Nikos gave me nothing. He certainly gave me no coin.''

"But he did, *mou* Jani. He did.''

"A coin?''

"A gold solidus. A very ancient coin.''

"But I would remember that. A gold coin . . . I—I couldn't have forgotten something like that.''

"You do not know, is all. Nikos, he put it in your house.''

"But why? What does it mean? Whose coin is it?''

"Why? Because he thought with you it would be safe.''

"Safe," she choked. "Someone wants to kill me for it. What is so important about this coin?''

Demir was silent for so long that she thought he had not understood the question. She was about to repeat it when he replied, "It is only an heirloom, Jani, belonging to our family. You see, Nikos was my cousin."

Janelle sat unmoving for several long seconds. "I—I didn't know that," she said, adding weakly, "I am so sorry."

"Yes." He picked up his cup of dark coffee and took a drink. "That is why he wanted me to have the coin."

"Is that why he was . . . killed? Because of a coin?"

"Yes."

"But why?"

"You see, *mou* Jani, this coin, it is like a key. It can open a door."

"To what?"

He hesitated, as if carefully weighing his words. "Nikos's father and my father had entrusted some heirlooms with another brother a long time ago. That brother, an uncle of mine, later joined the monastery at Karoulia. Phillipi gave up all worldly possessions. Now, you see, my father and Nikos's father have died, and Phillipi is the only one who knows where these family treasures are stored. You must understand, Jani, that we are simple people. Our needs are very small. A goat, a family, a glass of ouzo in the evenings and friends to play cards with in the cafés. We do not need much money. You understand this, yes?"

Janelle nodded.

"But alas, Nikos's mother has grown very ill. She needs most badly to be sent to your country for . . ."

He was searching for the word, so Janelle provided it. "Treatment."

"Yes, treatment. That takes money, Jani. Nikos was going to sell the family heirlooms to—to obtain that money." He paused for a moment and let his gaze drift out over the cliffs. "Now that he is gone...I must do this for his mother—my aunt."

Janelle was watching him closely, marveling at his slow, even tone. Zafer had been speaking with little inflection, as if he were reciting the much-practiced lines of a bard who had grown bored with his tale. Yet she knew there were two reasons for this. One was that he was not completely comfortable with her language. Each word had to be carefully considered before it was spoken. Then, too, he was a man who would not show much emotion. That, perhaps, could be taken as a sign of weakness, and everyone knew that Greek men had no weaknesses. So Janelle listened and understood and sympathized.

"And the coin? You said it was a key."

"Yes. The three men had a...how do you say when they talk something over and form a..."

"A plan? An arrangement?"

"Yes. That is it. An arrangement. The coin was to be used as identification. The brother, you see, had never seen Nikos or myself. And so, if we were to come to him and ask for the heirlooms..." Zafer shrugged. "He would not know whether to give them to us or not."

"But how would he know if it was the right coin? Surely it's not the only gold solidus."

"No, there are others. But this particular one is different. In the place where Constantine's eye should be, there is a gem. It was—how do you say?—stuck in there."

"Embedded."

"Yes, that must be the word. Embedded long ago into the coin. No other coins have been found like this one. It was to be used as a sign to the brother that we should have the heirlooms. Because of the gem embedded in the coin, he would know it was the right one.''

Janelle drank her nectar and thought about what Nikos's cousin had said. It made sense, up to a point. "I still don't understand the phone call I received. If this was only a family matter—''

"The family antiques are very valuable," Zafer interjected quickly. "Someone else has found this out. I asked you about the voice, because he has threatened me, also. This man Ivanov wants the coin because he knows it is the only way to get my uncle to give him the family treasures.''

"Zafer..." Janelle hesitated before continuing. "They are saying that Nikos was a thief. Is it true?''

"Yes.''

Janelle could only stare at him. How could she not have known the truth about Nikos? She sighed. "Then why didn't he steal to get the money for his mother? If she is that ill...''

"He would have, if I had not suggested this other way," Zafer countered. "So you see, Jani, his death..." He stared out over the square. "Because of my suggestion...I...I am responsible. I killed Nikos.''

"No, Zafer! You mustn't feel that way. You aren't responsible. You only tried to get Nikos to do what was right. It was probably that man Boris. Perhaps *he* is the one who killed Nikos!''

Demir stared down at his hands, clasped together on the table. "Perhaps so, Jani.''

She wanted to cry again, but for some reason the tears would not come. Maybe she had none left. Maybe all there was room for was anger at this person who had taken a life, and sadness for Zafer and Nikos's mother. She looked steadily at him and nodded slowly. "I will find this coin for you. I will try my best."

He smiled gently at her now. "Thank you, Jani. It is in your house. That much I believe. You must think where Nikos might have put it...a place where it would be very safe."

"I will try."

"I can ask for no more than that. And now," he said, "I must go."

"But how will I get in touch with you? Do you have a telephone here?"

His smile held a broad shade of wistfulness. "There is only one telephone for the six hundred residents who live in Olimbos. And so my answer is no, you cannot call me here. But I will be in contact, Jani. Of that you can be sure."

With one final smile, Zafer Demir stood up and walked away from the café. Janelle watched him go, the curious wet squish of his boots fading as he disappeared down the narrow, sloping street.

Chapter Six

It was dark when Janelle returned to Athens. The sky above the city had that peculiar sallow haze that prohibited the sight of even a single star. In contrast to the gentle afternoon on Karpathos, Athens was all loud voices, blaring horns and an endless cacophony of noise.

Janelle carried her small canvas haversack through the airport lobby, where the questions of bewildered tourists and the shouts of eager taxi drivers volleyed back and forth. Once outside, she hurried down the sidewalk, thinking that she saw an available taxi across the street. She had just stepped over the curb when a pair of headlights came into her peripheral vision. Bright, blinding lights, barreling down on her. She screamed at the same instant that a young man reached out and yanked her back toward the curb. She lost her balance and slipped, landing in the gutter.

English, Greek, French and a dozen other languages, it seemed, buzzed around her. She could respond to none of them. She could only stare mindlessly at the street along which the huge black car had just sped. In that split second before the man had pulled her to safety, in that instant when she'd known she was going to die, she had seen the car clearly. Her terrified gaze had locked on the front license plate. And what she had seen was unmistakable.

Janelle couldn't find her breath, couldn't find any words to speak, so she sat on the curb and stared straight ahead while the crowd of people closed around her, speaking in unintelligible tongues.

Through the madding throng, another hand reached down for her and grasped her arm. She looked up into Alec Hayden's face.

She started to cry, but a laugh came out instead. It died the moment it hit the air. Alec's expression killed it. He was glaring at her, his face a mask of frozen anger. He dragged her up and along behind him, flinging open the back door of a taxi and thrusting her inside. As soon as the door had closed behind him, he turned and glared at her once more. "Where the hell have you been?"

She was too stunned to answer for several long seconds. She could only repeat his name.

"You left Athens, for God's sake! What the hell is the matter with you? Don't you realize what that means? Don't you know the police are watching every step you take?"

"I—I was almost run over," she whispered, bewildered by his anger at her and by a world she no longer understood. "That car—it tried to—he meant to run me down!"

Alec stared at her, his mouth tight, his breath coming out of his nose in short, agitated bursts. "You look terrible."

The tone in his voice grated against her nerves, and her own anger began to surface. Dammit, she had almost been run over! Then Alec Hayden had practically wrenched her arm loose from its socket when he'd grabbed her and thrown her into the taxi, and now he was glaring at her as if she had personally ruined his day. "Thanks ever so much!" she snapped.

"I meant that you look . . . tired, gaunt."

"I haven't been eating too well. In case you hadn't noticed, I've had a few other things on my mind."

The car was moving away from the airport, but she was too drained to be aware of anything but the most peripheral of sensations. Besides, she simply didn't care.

"Why did you leave Athens, Janelle?"

"How did you know?"

He snorted. "Everyone knows."

She looked startled. "No one followed me. I was careful."

He laughed derisively. "Obviously not careful enough. Frank notified the police that you were going to meet with that man Demir. They've been looking for him and they wanted you to lead them to him. So yes, you were followed. And you're just damn lucky the police let me get to you before they did. God," he spat, "how *could* you have done it? I put my reputation on the line for you. I gave the authorities my word that you wouldn't leave. My word, dammit! And now you've made me look like a horse's ass."

"So now it's *your* reputation we're supposed to be worried about!"

"That's right. I've got a hell of a lot more to lose."

"I doubt that," she sneered. "And why aren't you in Turkey?"

"I was. I'm back."

She turned away from him and stared through the window at the steady stream of blaring traffic. "I was almost run over, you know," she said to the window.

This time, his voice was softer. "I know."

She turned toward him. "I saw the car."

His eyes narrowed, but that was the only change in his expression.

"I've seen it before."

He didn't say anything. He just continued to watch her closely.

"It belongs to the Russian embassy."

"And you think some Russian diplomat was trying to run you down?"

"I don't think so. I know so."

"Why?"

"I don't know, but I intend to find out."

"Janelle, listen..." Alec glanced at the back of the front seat and chewed on the inside of his lip. If there was a connection between this incident and Nikos's dealings with the embassy, he wanted it kept quiet until he knew for sure what was going on. If and when the time was right, then something could be said. "Don't mention anything about almost being run over—not to anyone."

"What? Are you crazy? How can you expect me *not* to say anything about it?"

The look he gave her was cold and hard. "I'm not asking you. I'm telling you." He saw the indignation burn in her eyes, so he spelled it out. "If you want my help—which you are most definitely going to need tonight—you have to do what I say. And I'm telling you not to say anything about it to anyone."

Her expression grew wary. "Why do you assume I'm going to need your help tonight?"

"Bluminfeld wants to see you."

Her lungs seized up. "He—he knows—that I left the city?"

"He knows."

"Oh, God." Her job. She had blown her entire career in just the first week of work. Everything she had worked for. Everything her parents had planned for. Gone. "Wh—what did he say—I mean, when he realized I was gone?"

Alec regarded her for a long moment. "You don't want to know."

IT WAS A GAME of dodge ball, and she was "it." The players who surrounded her were James Eddington Bluminfeld, Frank Osborn, Dimitris Heraki, an inspector with the Athens police, and Alec Hayden.

"Why, Janelle? Why!" Of all of them, it was James Bluminfeld's shrill voice that had the most impact on her. He was the one who, with the stroke of a pen, could end her foreign service career forever.

She felt the heat from each man's stare, and she could hear Alec translating softly to the inspector. "I received a phone call. Yesterday." Her accusing gaze jumped to Frank. "I told you what I was going to do." She looked back at Bluminfeld. "I was threatened, sir. I talked to Mr. Osborn about it."

"Yes," Bluminfeld murmured dryly. "I know. He told me."

Janelle tempered her hostility for the chief of security and stared down at the floor. "I was frightened, sir," she said to the chargé. "I knew I could trust Zafer. He was a friend . . . a cousin of Nikos."

The inspector stopped Alec's translation to say something. Then Alec, not even looking at Janelle, spoke the words in English to the group of men. "He could not have been a cousin. Zafer Demir is not Greek. He is a Turk."

Janelle, stunned, shook her head. "But—but he told me that—"

The inspector, firing off a string of questions that Alec did his best to answer, said something else. Suddenly everyone in the room was silent, all eyes trained on Janelle.

She looked at Alec and couldn't pull her gaze away. Something had happened. Something had been said. In that split second, everything had changed. But she had no idea what or why. The silence was palpable.

It was Alec who finally spoke, his voice low and hesitant. "You went to see this man Demir. Is that correct, Janelle?"

Her eyes jumped from one man to the next before returning to Alec. "Yes."

"And you met with him where?"

"In Olimbos, on—on the island of Karpathos."

"And what did he tell you?"

She stared at him for a long moment, agonizing over what to say. Zafer had told her that the family heirlooms were valuable. He had been threatened, also. How many people knew about the coin and the uncle who lived in a monastery? How many people would try to take away his family's treasure? God, she didn't know what to believe or whom to trust. Had Zafer lied to her? And what did she know about any of these men in this room? She had trusted Frank Osborn, and he had turned her in. Alec had gotten her released from jail, but it was obvious that he didn't believe fully in her innocence. Bluminfeld looked as if he would like nothing better than to see her behind bars, the embarrassing dilemma erased from his busy docket. Dimitris, who was standing in as vice-consul, most assuredly did not like the fact that Alec had taken over his position. Perhaps he felt it was a demotion of sorts and that it was all her fault.

"He told me that he was Nikos's cousin," she said.

"You already told us that, Janelle." Alec's eyes remained squarely on her face. "And the inspector has said that Demir and Nikos were not cousins. Now what else?"

She hesitated. "He—he said that Nikos was killed over some family heirlooms."

"And you believed that?"

"I had no reason not to."

"Did he ask you to give him something?"

"Well, yes, he, uh, said there was a—a coin that belonged to his family."

"Did you give it to him?"

"No. I don't have it."

"Did he threaten you?"

"No! Why would he do that?"

"No arguments between the two of you? No veiled threats?"

"No!" she repeated. She glanced around at the still faces again, at the eyes that were boring relentlessly through her. "Why are you asking me this? What is happening?"

Alec didn't answer. It was Bluminfeld who spoke. "The police received word a little over an hour ago that a body was washed up on the rocks at the base of Karpathos. The body was bloated and the face battered beyond recognition, but the police had reason to believe it was Zafer Demir."

Janelle didn't move. Every fiber of her being was frozen in an airless void. This wasn't happening. Not again. Not Nikos and Zafer both. She looked at the men around her. No one was paying any attention to her. They were all listening to something the inspector was saying.

Then Dimitris turned to her, his voice accusing. "The police say that you were the last person to see Zafer Demir alive."

She stared at the Greek diplomat and frowned, at first not comprehending. But finally the significance of his statement came through the barriers her brain had erected. She now understood perfectly what he was trying to tell her. "You—" a nervous chuckle of disbelief came from her throat "—you think that I..."

No one said a word for what seemed like an eternity. Finally Alec Hayden spoke directly to Bluminfeld. "You don't seriously believe that she could have killed him."

Bluminfeld stepped over to his desk and poured himself a glass of water. He took a drink, fumbled in his jacket pocket for a bottle of pills, then stuck it back. "I don't know what to think anymore." Janelle noticed that he would not look at her as he spoke. "Miss Lindsey has only been with us for one week. Her record states that she is of good moral character, but then this is, of course, her first foreign service assignment. Now, the fact that her father..." There was no need for the chargé to finish his sentence. Everyone there was aware of Janelle's background. No one wanted to be the first to accuse the daughter of a diplomat of being a felon.

"She was with Zafer Demir today," Dimitris repeated. "Still..." Even he did not want to come right out and say it. One of his jobs as acting vice-consul was to keep Americans out of jail, not get them thrown inside. And although he felt that, because of the State Department's interest, Alec Hayden had usurped all of his power in this case, Dimitris still didn't want to be the first to point the finger.

James Bluminfeld walked over to the bar sink against the wall and washed his hands. Twice. When he turned around, he spoke in Greek to the police inspector, but Janelle knew what he had said. His actions spoke more clearly than his words ever could have. He was washing his hands of Janelle Lindsey. The gendarmerie were free to arrest her and charge her with the murder of Zafer Demir.

Her gaze jumped to Alec, but he had turned toward the window, his expression hidden from her view. She had no idea what he was thinking. The inspector nodded to Bluminfeld and took a step toward her. A current of electricity ran through her body. She had always been so good. So polite to grown-ups, so obedient to authority. She had been a model child. Everyone had thought so. Everyone had said she would go far in life.

No one had said anything about jail. No one had hinted that her life would plummet to these depths. What would her mother say when she found out? She didn't like scandal and certainly wouldn't tolerate it in her own daughter. Scandal did not have a place in her social arena.

The inspector took Janelle's arm, but hesitated as he glanced once again at Bluminfeld.

"Please," the chargé said. "I don't believe there is any reason to cuff her. She will follow procedure and do the proper thing."

Janelle looked over at Alec again, but his back was still to her, his hands thrust into the pockets of his slacks. He had abandoned her. She was on her own.

Flanked by the inspector and Frank Osborn, Janelle stepped into the corridor and walked in a daze toward the embassy's front reception area. The building was very quiet. All of the secretaries and receptionists had gone home. She could hear the heavy footsteps of the men beside her, and she concentrated on the light tap, tap of her sandals on the linoleum floor. A marine guard held the front door open for them.

It was cooler tonight than it had previously been, and there was a moist breeze in the air. Janelle took a deep breath, but the smell of pollutants filled her nostrils.

The inspector's car was parked to the left of the entrance. Standing beside it were two other policemen. To the right was a panel that controlled all of the sophisticated electronics that were used to protect the compound from any terrorist threat. Janelle watched as the Marine guard on duty pushed a button to open the huge iron gate that spanned the driveway. She wondered vaguely what he thought of this woman who was being led from the embassy by a policeman and the head of the embassy's security. Did he care? Or did he just do his job and mind his own business?

Janelle had not formulated a plan. She was positive she hadn't had the time or the presence of mind. But something hot and electrifying had switched her into automatic gear. Without even considering the consequences of what she was doing, and giving no thought to the policemen and the marines with powerful, deadly guns behind her, she ran.

The iron gate was swinging open to allow their car to leave. She didn't hear the voices shouting behind her. She didn't look back to see Bluminfeld and Alec standing on the front steps watching her. She concentrated only on getting through that front gate before it swung shut.

The marine was obviously on top of the situation; he had quickly pressed a button to speed the closure of the gate. Janelle ran as fast as her legs could carry her, managing to slip through the slim opening only seconds before the gate had closed. She didn't wait around for it to open again so that the men chasing her could get out. She wasn't going to wait around for anything.

She heard someone curse, but she didn't bother to try to place the voice. Too many unrelated sights and sounds and smells were crowding into her brain. The moist air was so thick with pollutants, her eyes began to water, clouding her vision. She ran down the sidewalk past other embassies, museums and large mansions, heading straight across Zapio Gardens toward Syntagma Square. Losing herself in the crowds would be her only chance for escape.

A dog darted out from behind a bush and chased her, barking and nipping playfully at her heels. Janelle stopped only long enough to scream at it, and then she took off again. A taxi speeding down Leoforos Street narrowly missed her as she stepped off the curb. Horns blared, and the smell of exhaust was almost overwhelming. She felt as if her lungs would explode from fear and from the choking odors. But Janelle didn't stop. She couldn't.

Plunging through the crowds in Syntagma she ducked between the sweetshops and traversed an almost endless maze of short, dark alleyways and narrow streets. Music came from the tavernas; so did the smells of food, drink and sweat. The night air was like a curtain that she hacked and thrashed her way through.

Janelle knew the men were behind her, and she was amazed that they had not yet caught up with her. She heard isolated shouts but didn't know if they came from those pursuing her or from the nighttime revelers in the cafés. Feet pounded on the pavements all around her. Frantically she began to wonder if she was going in circles. Hadn't she passed this same pastry shop before? Hadn't she seen that young man and woman a few minutes ago? Janelle ducked down another alleyway, clutching her side as she ran. Her heart was pounding so hard, she was afraid it might not be able to take the strain. She wasn't in bad shape, but she wasn't used to running in marathons, either.

Thank God for the night, she thought breathlessly when she could run no more. She scurried beneath a stone staircase, squeezing far back into the corner. Footsteps sounded above her, men's shoes clattering their way down to the street. She closed her eyes and pressed her face into her drawn-up knees. It struck her now, really for the first time, just what she had done. She had run away from arrest. She was a fugitive from the law. She, Janelle Lindsey—model child, straight-A student, diplomatic aide, a loyal government servant—was an accused felon on the run.

The shouts from the newsboy at the corner kiosk and the steady grind of heavy traffic nearby made her only too aware of how unprotected she was. So far, the darkness had covered her escape. But what about when the night was over? What would she do then?

The smells of garlic and meat cooking in one of the tavernas made her realize how long it had been since she had eaten. She'd taken a few bites of the *tirropita* Zafer had bought for her in Olimbos, and before that she couldn't even remember the last full meal she'd had. However, she couldn't think about food now. She had to plan where to go. She had only a small amount of cash with her. The rest was back at the house. If she could get to Kolonaki... No, the police would be swarming all over Professor Goulandris's house like bees on a hive. But somehow she would have to go there to get some money and some clothes. Maybe later tonight she could slip in unnoticed. For now...

She scooted closer to the edge of the stairs and peered out at the street. The square was alive with the sounds of music and laughter. The breeze jostled the hanging lamps and sent the reflected light dancing across the square. In the small taverna just across from her, a young man was playing a guitar. The tune was gut-wrenching, soulful, a lonely sound that ripped through Janelle and made her realize that for the first time in her life she was all alone in the world.

After a while the music changed, the tempo increased and the rhythm grew lively as a three-piece band began to play. An elderly couple started to dance, and soon a crowd had gathered on the sidewalk, their feet lifted high, their hands touching their toes. A young man with a cigarette hanging loosely from his lips stretched his arms wide, snapped his fingers to the beat and then began to spin and squat and leap, kicking one leg high over the head of the young pregnant woman who was clapping her hands beside him. The band members held out their hands to catch the drachmas being tossed from the appreciative crowd. In Greece, this exuberant emotion was known as *kefi*, a spontaneous moment when spirits and well-being were at their peak.

Janelle watched from the dark beneath the stairs. She was all out of *kefi*.

ALEC TUNNELED THROUGH the thick, overgrown pines and crouched beneath the living room window. A sliver of light edged through the slit in the curtains. He wondered if she was in there. He had been waiting for hours until the police left, hoping she would come back here, but so far he had not seen her. She was out there somewhere, hiding in the twisted maze of Athens, scared, alone... He pushed the concerns aside. He had to find her for reasons of his own, which had nothing to do with what she was experiencing. He needed that coin. And at this point, Janelle Lindsey was the only one who might know where it was.

He heard a rustling in the bushes not too far away and coming closer. Hardly daring to breathe, he carefully wedged himself between a large pine tree and the house. His eyes were accustomed to the dark now, and he could see the movement as well as hear it. The shrubs parted slowly and cautiously; whoever was there was trying to make the least amount of noise. The rustling drew closer, and from the light through the curtains he could just make out a patterned fabric. Janelle's dress. The same one she had been wearing when he picked her up at the airport earlier. Like a man's oversize shirt, it stopped just above her knees and was belted at the waist. She wore the sleeves rolled up to her elbows.

She pushed through the shrubs and stopped, as if she, too, heard something. Alec hadn't moved, so he knew it wasn't he who had made her stop to listen. But after a moment, she seemed reassured and pressed on. She was within three feet of him now and she paused again, this time to look through the window. He waited. If he made his presence known right then, she might scream and run. If she would only come a little closer.

She dropped back down below the window and sat still, thinking. Then, slowly, she crept forward until she could have reached out and touched the top of Alec's shoe. He had to make his move now, before she saw him and uttered some sound that would give them both away.

He was directly behind her, so he reached out and in one swift movement wrapped an arm around her chest, holding her arms to her sides, and clamped the other hand tightly over her mouth. She tried to scream, but the sound was muffled by his hand as it pressed firmly against her lips. She squirmed in his arms and fought like a trapped animal. Her teeth edged over one of his fingers and bit down hard. Alec threw her to the ground, most of his weight on top of her, and felt the breath rush from her lungs.

He whispered in her ear, but Janelle was fighting too hard to hear him. He had to keep her quiet. That was the most important thing. He pressed himself down harder on her until she was unable to move at all. Her body sagged suddenly; all of the fight seemed to dribble away. Alec thought he heard a soft sob come from her throat. The sound cut through him like a knife.

"Shh. Janelle, it's Alec. You've got to be quiet." He felt no movement beneath him, so he eased his weight off her and loosened his hand from her mouth. His finger was wet with blood where she had bitten it, and it was starting to sting like crazy.

A small whisper sounded very close to the ground. Alec gathered Janelle up and turned her toward him. With gentle fingers, he carefully picked the pine needles from her hair. Dirt was caked on her cheek, and her lips were swollen and red from the pressure of his hand. She started to say something, but when he made a movement to quiet her, she flinched.

"I'm not going to hurt you, Janelle."

She brought a shaky hand up to her face and brushed back another strand of hair. "You already have."

Her body sagged, and Alec absorbed its weight. They stayed this way, leaning against each other, for a long moment. Finally he released her, whispering, "Don't you realize the police have been all around here? I just didn't want you to get shot."

She clamped her mouth shut and stared at the ground, refusing to hear him or even to see him.

"What were you planning to do," he demanded furiously when she wouldn't respond, "hide in the bushes for the rest of your life?"

She lifted her eyes to his face but saw that he wasn't looking at her. He was gazing out through the shrubs. "I don't really see any point in talking about it anymore," she said. "It's over. You'll be the big hero now, when you turn me over to the authorities."

He continued to scan the yard and the street, then glanced back. "What did you say?"

"I hope they give me solitary confinement."

He frowned at her for a second, then grasped her arm to lift her. "Come on, we've got to find a safe place." She tried to yank her arm away, but he held her fast. "What are you doing?" he growled.

"I'm, well—what are *you* doing?"

"I told you. I'm taking you somewhere to hide."

Janelle held her body rigid and refused to move. "I don't believe you."

He glanced toward the street again before he said, "Who the hell got you released in the first place?"

"Bluminfeld. You said you had no authority here."

"I lied."

"Are you lying now?"

"Look, Janelle, you have to trust someone. If you're caught—which you most assuredly will be if you go it alone—you'll be arrested. That is, unless they shoot you first for fleeing." Her wary expression had not budged. He grasped both of her upper arms. "Listen to me," he whispered. "I have used up all my favors. You will not be released again. And at this point Bluminfeld is ready to lock you up and throw away the key. Now, do you understand what I'm saying?"

Her chin was held high as she stared up at him, but it took all of her effort not to cry. She nodded.

"Okay." He sighed. "Now, do you also believe that I want to help?"

Her lower lip was beginning to quiver. She shook her head.

Alec expelled a breath of frustration.

"Do I have any choice in the matter?" she whispered.

"There is always a choice, Janelle. But I don't much think you'll like the alternative, which is to rot your life away in a foreign prison. You'd never survive it."

"Some choice," she mumbled.

He took one hand off her arm and brushed at the remaining pine needles that still clung to her hair. "My point exactly."

Chapter Seven

"Here, drink this. Come on. It will do you good."

Janelle took the glass of red wine from Alec's hands and drank deeply. It tasted wonderful and slid smoothly down her throat.

She glanced about the warm, shabby hotel room. It was small and smelled rather musty. The wood floor was bare except for a moth-eaten area rug. There was an old-fashioned pedestal sink on one wall, but the bathroom was down the hall. A light bulb hung from a single wire in the center of the ceiling.

"What if someone looks here? They'll find me. Or is that the plan?"

Alec, appearing more at ease and even more handsome in his faded jeans and cotton shirt rolled up at the cuffs, was standing at the window, holding the curtains aside as he looked down at the street two floors below. He turned at her question and dropped the curtains back in place. "Plan?"

"Yes. The way you're hoping to frame me. You're to be nice to me until I admit everything, and then you can turn me over to the police, right?"

An image flashed through his mind as he looked at her—a braid coming down, a smile, a hot dark night.

A dream that would not fade away. The flame licked through him even as he tried to deny its existence. "That's not how I operate."

"Oh?" she said shakily, suddenly intimidated by the disturbing sensations this man evoked in her. "Then how do you operate?"

"I like to think that I don't." He examined her smoky brown eyes for a long moment. Moist eyes. Eyes that were melting, that melted him. "You still don't believe I'm trying to help you, do you?"

She looked down at the glass clutched between her hands. "I don't know what to believe anymore. You say you're with the State Department, and—and James Bluminfeld obviously trusts you, but...well, why aren't you turning me in? Why aren't you following proper procedure like everyone else does?"

He walked over to the bedside table, picked up the wine bottle and tipped it back to take a long drink. She watched a trickle of it run down his chin. When he wiped it with the back of his wrist, she saw the dried blood on his finger where she had bitten him. Still holding the bottle, he sat down next to her on the edge of the bed. "Miss Lindsey, I have never in my life done anything according to procedure. And I certainly don't intend to start now."

His voice was as warm and full-bodied as the wine that coursed through her. And even more intoxicating. "But why are you doing this for me? Why should it matter to you if I'm free or not?"

Alec poured more wine into her glass, stalling—it seemed to her—for time. "Because I need your help."

"Mine?"

He hesitated again. "I came to Athens to meet with Nikos Marinatos. He had something for me. But he was killed first."

"The coin?"

"More than just that."

Janelle frowned at the cryptic answer. "Why you? How did you know Nikos?"

"It doesn't matter at this point."

"Doesn't matter? What is it, some sort of state secret?"

"Of sorts."

She groaned. "Oh, this is too confusing! I don't understand any of it." She studied the man sitting beside her. The light from the ceiling cast a white pool onto the top of his head. His eyes were a darker gray tonight and clouded. She wished she knew what he was thinking. She wished she knew more about him. The wine had made her feel looser inside, more mellow, her thoughts warmer and less direct. She was still wary of him, and yet . . . he didn't seem very menacing. He really was such an attractive man, strong yet gentle, too. Out of all the people at the embassy who could have helped her but didn't, only Alec had fought the legal system for her and saved her from recapture; now he was providing her with good wine and a warm place to stay. She remembered vividly the feel of his hands in her hair when he'd picked the dry pine needles from it. "May I ask you something, Mr. Hayden?"

"Sure."

"Do you think I killed Nikos and Zafer?"

He took another swig from the bottle, then wiped his mouth with the back of his hand again. "I think you can help me find out who did."

"Funny," she mused. "You didn't say no."

"About what?"

"I asked you if you thought I was guilty of murder, and you didn't say no."

His eyes traveled leisurely over her face, warming her, and he appeared as if he was going to move closer. She almost wished for one brief moment that he would. He didn't. "No, I don't think you killed them."

Her breath escaped in a sigh. "Thank you," she said, sitting back once more against the pillows. "I'm not sure how I can help you, though."

"You can tell me everything you know about them both—and you can help me find the coin before anyone else does."

Janelle had always been a trusting soul. Certainly she had always believed what the people in authority told her. But now all that had changed. She didn't know whom to believe anymore, whom to trust. "Why didn't you want me to tell anyone about the car that almost ran me down?"

"Because the driver may be the murderer."

"Boris," she whispered, the single breathless word encased in awe. "He—is that the name of the Russian diplomat?"

Alec nodded slowly.

Janelle shook her head. "I just can't believe it. A Russian diplomat! But if that's true, why didn't you want me to say something? They could arrest him, and I would be free."

"That would ruin everything."

She stared at Alec. "Why do you give me answers filled with riddles and double-talk that mean absolutely nothing? Why can't you just tell me what your involvement in this is?"

"The less you know, the safer you will be."

"Safe? I hardly think that word has any relevance to my present state, do you?"

"Still . . ."

Janelle sighed. He wasn't going to budge, and she wasn't sure how far to push him. After all, you didn't bite the hand that was feeding you. He said he needed her help. But then what? Perhaps once he had it, he would no longer care what happened to her. At that point, he could turn her over to the authorities and be done with her. So much was hidden behind those impenetrable eyes of his.

With another sigh, she stood up and, carrying the glass of wine, walked over to the window at which Alec had been standing only moments before. She knew he was watching her. She could feel his piercing eyes examining every facet of her being. Self-consciously she brushed at her cotton shirtwaist dress. She had washed her face and hands, but she thought she probably still looked like a mess.

She flipped aside the worn curtain and peered down at the quiet, dark street below. They were in the Plaka, the old quarter of the city; that much she knew. The twisting maze of streets was much like her thoughts at the moment, disoriented and convoluted, leading only to dead ends. "You know," she said with her back to the room, "I keep asking myself how this could have happened to me. I've always tried to do the right thing. Even when I wanted to be wild and crazy like everybody else, even when I was sick and tired of being so 'proper' all the time, I always did what was expected of me."

"Because of your father's position?"

She nodded but didn't turn around. "Yes."

"He was well liked in government circles, highly respected."

"Yes," she said. "I know."

"I only met him once when I was at the embassy in Paris a couple of years ago. I was really sorry to hear about his death. He seemed to be a very nice man."

She sighed. "Yes, well . . . everyone wanted to think that."

Silence filled the room. "You sound as if..." Alec's words faded away when she turned around and looked at him.

"My father had a private side, Mr. Hayden, nothing like his public one. He left the smiling, cordial man at work and brought home the dark, brooding one. No matter how hard I tried, I could never really please him. Oh, in front of other people he literally beamed over my accomplishments and showed nothing but pride and affection for me. But at home I heard only criticism. I—I don't think he liked me very much. I'm not sure why. And I shudder to think what he would say if he saw what I was involved in now!" She took a long drink of wine and rested her back against the wall.

Alec remained on the bed, watching her, suddenly assaulted by the vivid details of last night's dream. Something hot crawled through his veins and settled down low in his abdomen. This reaction wasn't like him. He wasn't the sort who mixed business with pleasure. And Janelle Lindsey was strictly business. "What about your mother?" he asked, needing a diversion.

"Do you mean, did she see his darker side?"

He nodded.

"Yes, but the compensation she received must have outweighed the disadvantages. She was a military wife first and foremost—straight down the line. She knew what her duties were, and she followed them to the letter. She was the perfect hostess, the perfect diplomat's wife. She loved the life."

"And your relationship with her?"

"It was . . . good, I guess. We didn't confide in each other or anything. I never felt I could tell her about too many personal things. But it was an okay relationship. Basically, she went Dad's way and I went Dad's way, and we all traipsed along like a flock of happy ducks."

"Where is she now?"

"Mother? She married some Hollywood producer a few months ago."

"You don't sound as if you approve."

"What's to approve or disapprove? It's her life. They have houses in Beverly Hills and Palm Springs, a co-op in New York. She says she's happy."

"Maybe she is."

Janelle shrugged. "Maybe. Oh, just listen to me! I sound like a neglected kid, feeling ever so sorry for myself. I don't usually indulge in this sort of thing."

Alec smiled. "We're all entitled to a little self-pity now and then. And you've been through a hell of a lot in the past couple of days. A weaker woman would have caved in long before now." He patted the bed. "Why don't you come and sit down?"

Janelle didn't move, but she took in everything about him in that moment—his face, his body, his eyes, the curve of his mouth. It was a strong face, determined and confident, and he was a man who looked a person squarely in the eye, who seemed to know that his vision of the world was the right one, the one the whole world should adopt. But his smile had a gentling effect on the rest of his face; it curved easily and revealed straight white teeth and more than a hint of warm sensuality. She liked looking at him. Tonight he appeared so safe, so warm. In fact, she almost felt more comfortable in his company than she had in anyone else's. But could she ever trust again—or had Nikos ripped that ability from her? Could she ever again find something to smile about?

Janelle pushed herself away from the wall and moved toward the bed. Alec had stacked up the pillows against the headboard for her, so she sat down and leaned back against them. The wine was starting to make her sleepy, but she knew that Alec would not allow her to sleep until she had given him some of the information he sought.

"I guess you have certain questions you want to ask."

His eyes trailed up the bare length of her legs to the hem of her dress. The heat swelled in his lower body, like a storm gathering strength. He forced himself to remember why he was here, why he had gotten her out of jail in the first place. "Why don't you just tell me about Nikos?"

"I don't really know where to begin," she said. After a substantial pause, during which he offered no help, she gave it a try. "I had never met anyone quite like him before. When I was in high school, my parents wouldn't let me date. And when I went to college, I was expected to keep up my grades, of course. On holidays, I always came home for whatever special functions were being held at the embassy." She let a sip of wine warm her body. "Maybe I'm making excuses for my behavior."

"What do you mean?"

"For having a—a physical relationship with a man I didn't know very well—for having one with the wrong man."

"You said you made love with him only once. Was that true?"

"Yes. But love? I don't know if love had much to do with it." Janelle laughed wryly. "It was more of a—a fling. I thought I was being terribly modern and sophisticated."

"And now?"

Her eyes closed briefly. "Now I realize how foolish I was."

"You said he was the wrong man, a man you didn't know."

"Yes. I thought I did at first. I told you he was charming. Well, that was an understatement. He washed over me like a twenty-foot wave. In a way it was exhilarating, and in another way, suffocating. I didn't have the experience for someone like him." She laughed again, this time with bitterness. "In truth, I think I wanted to fall for all the lines he fed me."

"Such as?"

"Oh, he was always telling me how beautiful I was." She shrugged. "Things like that."

Alec's eyes automatically swept over her face and down her body. "Why do you call that a line?"

She kept her gaze directed into her wineglass, confused by the feelings his quiet voice was stirring in her. "He also said he'd never met anyone iike me before."

"He probably hadn't."

"For a couple of days there in Vienna, he made me feel like I was the most important person in the world . . . and it had nothing to do with my father. It was me. I was important. I was just right."

Alec was quiet for a long time, but Janelle wouldn't look at him. "And when did you stop believing him?" he finally asked.

She sighed. "The morning after, if you'll excuse the cliché. He was different, changed. Almost a Jekyll and Hyde. I must say, it's not a very nice feeling to sleep with a man and then wake up the next morning and find out you've made a stupid mistake. When we were on the train from Austria, it was really bad. He became nervous and jumpy. He snapped at everyone— the porters, the bartenders, the ticket takers. Suddenly no one—certainly not I—could do anything right. That was also when he began to question me about everything."

"You mean about your job?"

"Yes."

"But you said he asked you a lot of questions that first night you met him . . . at the party."

"He did," she agreed. "But it was worse after we left Vienna. He started in all over again." Janelle frowned as the memory came back to her. "He was so insistent. And when I wouldn't tell him what he wanted to know, he accused me of deceiving him, of deliberately trying to destroy him." She looked at Alec. "I was shocked. *I* deceived *him*? He had it all backwards. And he wanted to know whose house I would be living in, where my office would be, how well I knew the chargé. He named several people on the staff and asked me how well I knew them. I don't know where he got his information. I never told him the name of the chief of security or the vice-consul or the staff assistants or anyone else. But he knew all of their names. Frank's, Dimitris's, Bluminfeld's, and a half-dozen others.''

"But he never got the information he wanted out of you?"

"Never. I have worked for years and years to get a position with the Foreign Service. I've lived among diplomats all my life. I know what is expected, what things can be talked about and what things cannot. I guess it says something about how frivolous my feelings were for him, but my first loyalty was to my position here in Greece.''

They were both silent for a few minutes. Janelle knew that Alec was watching her. She could sense his eyes upon her.

"What do you do at the embassy?" he asked.

She glanced up at him and smiled, grateful for the change of subject. "Oh, terribly important things. All very hush-hush, of course.''

He smiled back. "Of course.''

"Actually, I'm supposed to work directly for James Bluminfeld. I ready his quill pen with red ink and reel out all those miles and miles of red tape he's so fond of wrapping around everything. 'Staff assistant' is my title.'' She smiled down at her hands folded primly in her lap. "Facetiousness aside, I really did want this job, Mr. Hayden. It's very important to me.''

"Do me a favor," he said. "Don't call me Mr. Hayden. It makes me feel terribly old and proper.''

She cocked her head as she watched him pour her some more wine. "And are you?"

"Am I what?"

"Old and proper.''

He took a drink from the bottle and contemplated the question. "I'm thirty-seven, so—yeah, I guess I'm old—but definitely not proper."

She regarded him quietly. "Are you someone I can trust?"

His gaze narrowed. After a reflective pause, he lifted his hand toward her and slid his finger very slowly and deliberately along the curve of her mouth. His eyes followed the movement, and he spoke softly. "If I were you, Janelle, I wouldn't trust anyone."

She had closed her eyes while his finger engraved a path around her lips, and now that he had pulled his hand back and let it drop to the bed, she wanted the feeling to go on and on. His gentleness was such a surprise to her. She finally opened her eyes. "Are you married . . . Alec?"

The easy smile faded from his face. "I was."

"You're divorced, then?"

"Yes."

"What was her name?"

"Erin. Why do you want to know?"

His voice had lost its warmth and had a sharp edge to it. But still, she had to know. She knew so little about him, almost nothing about what he actually did for a living or what he was doing in Athens. If she could just learn this one small facet of his life. "I was interested, that's all."

He took another long drink from the bottle and stared at the worn rug on the floor. "She liked my trips away from home too much."

"She was . . . unfaithful?"

"That's a quaint way of putting it." He looked at her and shook his head, bemused. "You really are a good girl, aren't you, Janelle?"

"I don't know what you mean."

He was studying her with an intensity that was frightening. It was as if he actually wanted to know what made her tick, as if who she was and what she thought about things really mattered to him. But then the look faded, and he shook his head roughly. "Ah, hell, never mind. You didn't finish telling me about Nikos. What happened after he became so insistent?"

She stared down into her glass, embarrassed that the wine had made her see what wasn't there. "When we first arrived in Athens, he seemed okay, back to normal. I was in a strange city, and he was a friend. We went out a few times. He showed me around and didn't seem any more interested than I was in an intimate relationship. But then two or three nights ago... I don't know, I've lost track of time at this point. But anyway, one night this past week he grew... particularly strange. He got it into his head that I worked for the CIA or something and that I was here to spy on him. He started saying some cruel things to me, and he became physical—you know, kind of rough. I was scared. There was that split personality again, that irrational side of him that I didn't know."

Alec kept his voice tightly under control, but a hint of anger came through. "Did he hurt you?"

"I—I thought he was going to. So I told him as forcefully as I could to leave me alone." Janelle was quiet for several moments. "I told him I didn't want to see him anymore."

"And what did he say?"

"He sneered at me and said, 'We'll see about that.' That was the last time I saw him."

"Except when you walked into your house and found his body."

The glass she was holding tipped, and the wine sloshed onto the bedspread. Alec scooted closer and reached for the glass before it fell from her hands. "It's okay. Come on, relax." He set the glass on the table.

"There was so much blood and—oh, Alec, it was so awful!"

"Okay," he said softly, pulling her to him and holding her shaking body in his arms. "Forget it. Get it out of your mind."

"I've tried, really I have."

"I know. Listen, it's going to be okay." He helped her lean back against the pillows and brushed a few strands of hair away from her face. Her hair was more wavy than he had imagined. When she wore it in a braid, he couldn't tell if it was straight or not. But now that it was loose, he realized it was thick and curled gently at the ends.

The quivering inside Janelle slowly began to subside with each stroke of his fingers against her hair. She wondered why she had told him all the things she had, and why she felt that she could confide in him. After all, he too was a stranger, and she wasn't sure how reliable her judgment of people was right now. Still, there was a certain freedom in honesty. She let out a deep sigh. "I haven't helped you at all, have I?"

His hand moved back to the bedspread. "It's a start."

She smiled at him. "Thank you, Alec Hayden."

He cocked his head, surprised. "For what?"

"For being so nice to me."

His eyes narrowed in distrust of his own feelings. But then he leaned over, resting his hands on the opposite sides of her legs, his face very close, his mouth curving a little to the left in a reluctant smile. He said nothing. He wanted her to make the first move.

"I really do want to help you, Alec. I'm just not sure what questions you have."

His eyes skimmed over her face, lingering on her mouth. "We can talk about it tomorrow, Janelle."

She knew what he was suggesting. And she knew what she wanted him to do. But she couldn't let herself feel this way. She had given in to a physical nudge with Nikos, and it had turned out to be the biggest mistake of her life. Janelle wasn't sure exactly what it was that she felt for Alec Hayden, but whatever it was, it scared her. She felt too warm with him, too secure, too drawn to his slow, quiet appeal.

She shook her head slowly, almost sadly. "I think you'd better ask me some questions."

She couldn't tell if it was disappointment or relief in his voice when he finally said, "Okay, tell me about Zafer."

She stared at him for a long moment, regretting her decision, but she forced her thoughts on what he wanted to know. "He was the nicest man. Really Greek, you know. At least I thought he was Greek. Dark, swarthy..." She frowned. "You know, those were the oddest shoes..."

"Shoes?"

"Yes. His shoes were...squeaky sounding. I thought at first that he had been tromping around in mud or water or something. But the sky was clear. There had been no rain. I guess they just sounded that way."

"Squeaky?"

"Well, squishy."

"Go on," Alec prodded.

"Yes, well, I went to Karpathos, and they were having this celebration..."

"Why did you go there?"

"Because Zafer told me to."

"Why?"

It made her tired even to think about it. When was the last time she had slept? "I don't know. Maybe it was because he didn't want to talk about the coin over the phone."

"But he talked to you about the coin when you came to the island."

"Oh, yes." Janelle's tired gaze dropped to the bed beneath her. "He said I have it."

Alec's eyes narrowed in a close study of her face. "And do you?" he asked softly.

She shrugged and closed her eyes. "I don't know, Alec. I don't think so, but...well, he seemed so sure that I did."

"Did he tell you what the coin was to be used for?"

"He said it was the only way he could get to his family's heirlooms. His uncle, uh—what was his name? I forgot. Anyway, his uncle supposedly hid them, and now he's living in a monastery in Karoulia, but I don't know where that is."

"Mount Athos." Alec's brief smile at her had vanished and was replaced by a stern scowl. The gravity of this problem was weighing heavily on him. Janelle had the urge to reach up and lay her hand against his jaw, to soften the hard line. Without realizing it, she did just that.

Alec sucked his breath in and locked his eyes with hers. "Did Zafer say where he thought the coin might be, Janelle?"

"No."

"Try to think. Just for a minute. Did Nikos ever give you things—oh, you know, the things lovers give each other? Flowers, candy—anything? Any clue that might help."

"He never gave me anything except—except that beautiful figurine in Vienna—"

"Figurine? What figurine?"

She was staring at her fingers as they lifted as if by their own accord to stroke along the contour of his jaw.

Pulled as if by some invisible chain, Alec leaned toward her and she slid lower on the bed. His hands came up to rest against each side of her face. "Janelle." Her name on his lips sounded like liquid gold, and the flesh in her lower body pulsed to life. Very slowly and with great reluctance, his fingers tunneled into her hair and wrapped themselves around a thick strand, absorbing the feel of it. His face was only inches from hers, but still he held off, unsure.

"You don't want to kiss me, do you, Alec?"

His gaze slid from her closed eyes to her mouth. "No," he whispered, lowering his mouth to hers. "I don't." It was a gentle kiss, a first mating, not at all what she had expected from a man who only a few hours earlier had thrown her to the ground and pressed his weight upon her. Now, with his tongue, he tasted her lips, sampling her as if she were a delicacy that must be savored slowly and with great care. When she opened her eyes, his face was again only a few inches above her, and his eyes were lingering on the skin exposed at the top button of her dress.

His fingers trailed languorously down the length of her face and neck, following the line of her collar. At the top button, he hesitated, but only for a moment. The button slipped through the hole, his hand slid down, and the next button followed. His hand snaked inside the opening, and he felt her heart beating rapidly beneath his palm. When his hand closed over her breast, her eyes closed. God, but he wished he didn't want her so badly. This was not supposed to be. This was not the way it was supposed to happen. He had gotten her released from jail for one reason only. The coin. That was all he wanted. And yet . . . her skin was so soft, so smooth. "You feel so good," he found himself murmuring, and his mouth dropped down to taste the mounded flesh his fingers had found.

Her eyes were shut tight, but it wasn't to shut out what was happening. It was because she was afraid if she opened them, he would not really be holding her and kissing her breast and moving his hands over her the way he was. Janelle didn't want it to be a dream. She didn't want to open her eyes and discover that none of this was real. She wanted the fear to go away, but she wanted the feel of Alec Hayden to stay with her forever.

When he raised himself up, Janelle reluctantly opened her eyes. He was watching her, his breath rapid, his eyes full of indecision. And she knew that he had been honest when he said he didn't want to kiss her. He didn't. He wanted information. He wanted her help. Yet he was torn. She could see it in his eyes and feel it in his touch. When their eyes met, he looked as if he was going to kiss her again, as if he wanted to.

But instead, he spoke. "I have to know, Janelle. What figurine?"

So, she thought, cauterizing the wound quickly before it could spread. Okay, so that was all this had been about, all he really wanted. She had known that. He wanted information. "It's of a violinist," she answered, working hard to maintain an expression that would reveal nothing of what she was feeling or of the turmoil he provoked in her. "Actually, it's a music box. You wind it up and it plays 'The Emperor's Waltz.'"

"What is it made of?"

"Ceramic, I guess."

"Where do you keep it?"

She looked away from him. She didn't understand his insistence. She didn't understand him. "On my desk." Then, as if she had been smacked hard in the stomach, her eyes swung back to him and her mouth dropped open. "Alec!" She pushed him off her and sat up, pulling her dress closed. "Oh, my God, Alec!"

"What? What is it?"

She was staring across the room, her eyes wide, her heart pounding, her mind listening to the voices in her memory. "Nikos—yes, it has to be—he told me that someday that statue would be worth its weight in— *gold*, Alec! That's where it is. It has to be! It was right there, all along. They searched my house, but they never thought to look at the embassy—in my office!"

"You may be right, Janelle."

She sensed the excitement in him, even though she could tell he was trying to control it. "I am right, aren't I, Alec?"

He kissed her lightly on the forehead and stood up, grabbing his jacket off the back of a chair. "There's only one way to find out." He turned back to her. "I want you to lock the door behind me."

"You're going . . . now?"

"I've got to get it before someone else does."

"And once you have it?"

He stood beside the bed and stared down at her. A moment passed in silence. Then he said, "I'll come back, Janelle."

She wanted to believe him. She wanted to have trust and faith in him. She wanted to mean something more to him than merely a source of information. And yet he had told her not to trust anyone. Who was this Alec Hayden? Was he someone she could believe? She was scared to death for him to leave her here alone. There was a chance that he wouldn't come back. There was also a chance that the police might know where she was and that tomorrow might bring even more terror than tonight had.

She tried to still the fearful beating of her pulse and forced herself to look at him with steady eyes. "I'll lock the door behind you."

THE DREAM CAME TO HER in vivid color. Bright, blinding lights, red and yellow. The twin beams of a car's headlights. But there was nothing threatening about them. They were moving slowly toward her, beckoning her; when she drew closer, she realized they weren't headlights at all. They were Alec's eyes. Soft, gentle. He was watching her, smiling down at her, the gray of his eyes like a warm mist on a summer morn. His hands moved over her body in caressing, worshiping touches. But suddenly the bright lights grew brighter, and she was running, running from Alec and Nikos. They wanted to take her violin from her. They wanted to take the music away. They had guns and they began firing at her—warning shots, it seemed—but she didn't stop. She slipped over a fence and through a gate. A soldier aimed a rifle at her, but she gave him some gold coins and he was happy. She rounded a corner and ran into something hard. It was only Alec's body, and he was suddenly holding her, comforting her, while she sobbed into the warmth of his shirt.

Janelle woke up and found that her pillow was soaked with tears. She lay very still, listening to the sounds of the night beyond the window. She had no idea what time it was or how long she had been asleep. She wondered where Alec had gone. Her muscles ached from fatigue, and all she wanted was to sleep through the rest of the night without awakening.

She changed positions so that the disturbing dream would not come back to her. The sound of guitar music drifted up from the street below, its melody haunting in the silence of the room. Janelle shivered suddenly. She'd remembered that Alec had gone to the embassy to get the coin from her office.

And she remembered that she was a fugitive.

Chapter Eight

It was dark, too dark to see anything in front of them. The two men slipped through the narrow corridors with the caution and furtive steps of rats in search of food for the nest. The south transept of the church was just ahead, and they had to feel their way along the cool stucco walls. One of the men's heavy boots caught on the leg of a chair, and the scraping sound against the wooden floor echoed loudly. They stopped, held their breath and waited. When no circles of light shot down to capture them, when no door at the far end of the sanctuary opened to expose them, they moved on, set on completing the task. They were paid well for what they did. But beyond that, the thought of punishment, of what Boris Ivanov would do to them if they failed, spurred them on even when fear of capture closed around them and squeezed all breath from their lungs.

They passed the north apse and then groped their way into the transept. One of the men reached into his pocket and pulled out a thin flashlight. He flicked it on. It offered only a small pinpoint of light, which was all they needed or wanted. Very slowly, he moved the beam along the wall, covering every inch, stopping finally on a glass case. The sides of the case were bronze. Only the doors were glass. And the lock on it . . . yes, it would take some work. But they had dealt with more difficult locks.

The man with the flashlight held the beam steady while the other man stepped up to the case. He extracted a leather pouch from beneath his sweater, unzipped it and took out the tools he needed. After wiping away the sweat from his upper lip, he went to work. From start to finish, the job took less than fifteen minutes. The man with the flashlight watched his partner lift the silver chalice into his hands. They looked at each other and smiled. Boris would be pleased.

"THE ENTIRE SITUATION has gotten out of hand." James Bluminfeld glared across the desk at Alec. "I knew it would. I told you she might bolt. I was right all along. I told you. How *could* this have happened? I should never have listened to you . . ."

Alec sat patiently, waiting for the tirade to end. Frank, sitting next to him, had taken out his nail clipper and was clicking away. "The police will find her," Alex finally interjected.

"Police!" Bluminfeld sputtered. "The Greek gendarmerie! You must be joking." He shook his head. "No, she's gone, Hayden. And I'm holding you personally responsible. This was not my fault. You're the one who wanted her released—God only knows why. You're the one who's on the line for this."

"Fine, James. I'll take the heat. But I still think she'll show up sooner or later. As you said to the inspector, she'll do the proper thing. Let's face it, she's scared. Who wouldn't be?"

Frank looked up from his nails. "The police are over at her house now. They're hoping to find something that will point 'em in the right direction."

"I want to go through her office."

"I've already done that, Hayden," Frank said. "And so have the police."

"I know, I know. Hell, I probably won't come up with anything, but...well, you know how I am, Frank. I'd just like to take a look."

The head of security shrugged. "Okay by me."

"Good." Alec stood up, and Frank, after slipping his nail clipper into his pocket, stood up with him.

He pulled a chain of keys from his pocket. "I'll open it up for you."

Alec glanced down at Bluminfeld, who was drumming his tapered fingers against the polished rosewood desk. This case was really getting to him. He looked as if he was on the verge of tears. But then, this had been his big chance to move up the government totem pole. Taking over as chief of mission in the ambassador's absence had been a godsend. Then the fiasco with Janelle had come along. Alec didn't have much sympathy for the man, but at the same time he could understand what was going through Bluminfeld's mind. Yet as he looked down at the chargé d'affaires, all Alec could think of was what a pathetically weak creature James was.

Following Frank out of the office, Alec turned to the right and waited while Frank unlocked the door to Janelle's office. The door swung open, and the security chief stepped aside for Alec to enter. "You need any help?"

"No, Frank. I do better on my own. I'm sure I won't find anything, but then you never know."

"Tell me something, Hayden." Frank leaned against the doorframe.

Alec sat down on the corner of Janelle's desk and folded his arms. "What's that?"

"If this gal doesn't show up... well, ya know, you signing the release and all... what's going to happen to you?"

"One thing I've learned in the past few years, Osborn, is not to worry too much about the what ifs. When you do, you lose all sense of direction and action, and you end up like that." Aware that all offices in the embassy were bugged, his thumb waved in the direction of Bluminfeld's office. "Know what I mean?"

Frank laughed. "Do I ever." He turned to go, but stopped when Alec spoke again.

"But the truth is, Frank, if this thing isn't wrapped up pretty soon, I'll be in what you Texans like to call a heap of trouble."

"Go to it, then, boy. Let me know if you find anything."

Once he was alone, Alec closed and locked the door, then moved to the other side of the desk and sat down in Janelle's chair. He ran his hands over the smooth wood in front of him and stared at the small figurine that sat in one corner. He could see the coin wedged in between the miniature violin strings, but only because he knew it was there. It looked as if it were part of the musical mechanism, so unless you knew what you were looking for, you would never have noticed it. He didn't pick up the figurine yet. He just looked at it. Surveillance in an embassy compound was a way of life, and there could very well be a dozen cameras aimed right on him at this moment. He at least had to go through the motions of searching her desk.

He sat back in the chair and opened the top drawer. Inside were all the office essentials—stapler, pens, correction fluid, letterhead stationery, paper clips, calculator. He opened the deep drawer to the left and leafed through the files. Everything pertained to embassy business, but then he had known that it would. Janelle Lindsey was not the type to mix her personal life with her professional one. He suspected now that the dossier on her had not been incomplete. She really was as wholesome and straightlaced as it had indicated. The thought made him very uneasy. At times he felt as if he had seen everything and had done a good portion of it, too. But this particular woman threw him off balance at every turn. She brought out tender feelings and a need to protect that he didn't know he had. He wasn't at all sure he liked his new knowledge.

Alec got up and moved to the filing cabinet that stood against the wall. He made a perfunctory show of scanning each file. He was going to have to pick up the figurine and slip it into his pocket, but he hadn't yet figured out how to do it without being detected.

Pulling a stack of files from the third drawer, he carried them to the desk and plopped them down next to the violinist. Opening the first, he perused its contents and then dropped it on the other side of the figurine. After a few minutes, files covered the desk, and the figurine was drowning in a sea of paper. While methodically gathering up the files to put them away, he slipped the violinist into his jacket pocket, then stacked the files and put them back into the drawers, one by one.

He opened the door, glanced back once at the immaculately clean office, flipped off the light and stepped into the hall. Frank Osborn was coming down the corridor to meet him.

"Find anything, Hayden?" he asked as he bent over to lock the door.

Alec shook his head. "Not a thing. But I hadn't really expected to find much."

"Guess we'll have to see what the police come up with at her house."

"Guess so. Well, thanks for the opportunity, Frank."

"Sure, no problem. We'll keep digging. My daddy always said, if the oil's there, eventually you're gonna hit something other than a dry hole."

Alec stared at him for a long moment. "There's oil, Frank. It's there, and I'm going to find it."

SUNLIGHT ANGLED through the space between window and shade covering. The room was hot and stuffy and pulled Janelle, groggy and unwilling, from her sleep. Forcing her eyes open, she punched up the pillows behind her back and sat up. The room was dirtier than she had remembered it last night. The rug looked even more worn, the walls in great need of paint. And the lack of fresh air was almost suffocating. She had slept hard after the disturbing dreams finally ended, and she wasn't sure she was ready to face the uncertainty of a new day.

She let the dawn slip into her mind and body, but she let it in slowly. Glancing at the other half of the bed, she knew it would have been a shock if Alec had been lying there, but it was an even greater shock to realize that he was not. He was not even in the room.

But, of course, the bathroom was down the hall, so that was probably where he was.

She snuggled back into the pillows, not wanting to think about the terror of the past few days or the unpredictability of tomorrow. She simply wanted to close her eyes and drift. Just for a few more minutes.

After more than a few minutes, she woke up again and realized with a start that Alec had not come back. She tried to remember all that he had said last night, all that they had talked about. And it was with acute embarrassment that she remembered the personal things she had told him about herself, her relationship with her parents and her feelings for Nikos. Why had she done that? Why had she revealed so much to a perfect stranger?

And even more than that, she had kissed him and let him touch her. She had wanted his mouth and hands on her body. She had urged him to kiss and caress her. What was worse was that she had been disappointed when he stopped. What had happened to her sanity?

There was something about that man that made her feel so unsteady, so inadequate. Alec Hayden was so methodical, so sure of himself, while she was sure about nothing. She had broken down and cried in front of him. She had lost all control with him. He had been forced to comfort her. The fact that she felt so secure in his arms and wanted to stay within the warm enclosure of his body made her feel even more inadequate. What must he think of her? And why was he wasting his time with her?

She sank against the pillows. The figurine. Yes, her little musical man that played Strauss. She had told Alec all about it. And now she was convinced that the coin was hidden in it. Alec had gone to get it. That was why he was wasting his time with her. That was what he had been after all along. The last thing she remembered was that he had smiled down at her and walked out. And now he was gone. She had been duped again. Again. He had known exactly which of her strings to pull and how to get what he wanted.

She had to think. She had to figure out what to do next. No doubt, Alec Hayden had also tipped off the police as to where she was. Any minute now they would show up, burst through the door with handguns poised and cocked, and drag her off to the deepest, darkest dungeon they could find. She had to get away from here, but where could she go?

She tossed back the bedspread and had set one foot on the floor when she heard footsteps outside the door. Frozen, with one leg still on the bed, her fingers clutched around the frayed edge of the bedspread, she stared at the door as if she could see through it. They had come. The police were here for her. It was over.

Her gaze dropped to the doorknob as it began to turn. She heard the metal thrust of a key in the lock and then a resounding click. Slowly, the door opened.

Alec Hayden stood in the opening, a couple of sacks in his arms, the key stuck between his teeth. He paused before entering and frowned at her. "What's the matter? What happened?"

It took several long seconds before the blood returned to her face. It took even longer for her brain to start functioning again. "You weren't here. I—I thought you had left."

"I did leave."

"I mean . . . I thought you had . . . left."

Alec's eyes flicked to the bedside table, and Janelle's own gaze followed. There on the table beside her was the eight-inch-tall ceramic man with a violin tucked under his chin and the bow poised above the strings. The coin was wedged in behind the strings of the violin and looked as if it were an integral part of the musical workings.

"You think I would leave without that?" Alec asked.

Janelle could feel her face suffused with blood, but she tried valiantly to appear unruffled. She cleared her throat and found her voice. "No, I suppose you wouldn't."

Alec dropped the sacks on the bed. "Nikos Marinatos was a pretty clever fellow."

She shook her head, marveling. "It was there all the time. Right in front of me. I can't believe no one thought to look in my office."

"That often happens. You don't see things that are right under your nose or think of the obvious." He sat down on the bed. "I also made it to a store and bought some clothes for you. I hope I got the right things. I went mainly on the shopkeeper's say so."

Her gratitude outweighed her embarrassment. "Thank you, Alec."

"You're welcome."

"And now what?"

He smiled. "Now we eat." He took a loaf of bread and some tangerines from one of the bags. "You're probably starving."

"I am. I can't remember the last meal I had."

"Did you sleep well?"

She didn't want to tell him about her dreams. She had told him so much already, and she wasn't even sure where to draw the line between reality and unreality. "Like a log," she answered. "Where did you sleep?" She tried to make the question sound casual.

"I didn't get back here until about four, and then I lay down beside you for a little while." He was amused by her expression. "I too was very tired."

She watched him take a bite of a juicy tangerine and then caught the one he tossed to her. "What's in the other bag?"

"Oh, you're going to love this." He reached over and pulled it near, dumping a pile of black and gray material onto the bed. "I had to guess at the sizes, so I hope they're right. Now the shoes, I don't know..."

Janelle leaned over and extricated something from the pile. "What is it?"

"I think it's a skirt. That's what the shopkeeper said. Greek hours are wonderful. Where else could you buy clothes in the middle of the night?"

"You're kidding. I'm supposed to wear this?"

"Only if you want to get out of Athens undetected."

Janelle sifted through the remainder of the clothes. "This, I take it, is a scarf."

"Yes. And a must, I might add. Oh, and you'll have to button this sweater up, because I forgot to buy a blouse." He shrugged at her expression. "Sorry."

She drew out the shoes and some tights and held them up. "These must make the ensemble complete."

"A peasant woman in mourning. One of the more common sights in this part of the world."

Janelle sat very still on the bed, moving only her hand across the folds of the black material. She looked at Alec. "Why are you doing this for me?"

His eyes caught with hers, but he didn't answer.

"Is there more information you want?" she asked.

He looked away, but his gaze was drawn back to her. "In the beginning...at first, yes, that was the reason for getting you out of jail, for helping you, for hiding you last night."

"And now?"

Alec played with the tangerine pit in his hand, tossing it back and forth from one palm to the other. But his eyes remained squarely on Janelle's face. "You still haven't told me the name of Zafer's contact in Mount Athos."

"The one he called his uncle?"

"Yes."

"And once I tell you that, you are finished with me, is that it?"

His mouth tightened. "Don't make it sound like that."

"Why? It's the truth, isn't it? You needed me for information—and for the coin, of course. And now you'll pack me off in some peasant clothing, and I'll be on my own. You won't have to concern yourself with me anymore."

"There's a hotel in Volos. You'll be safe there until this business is wrapped up. I can give you the name of someone to contact if you need anything."

"I can take care of myself."

A cynical snort was his response to that.

Janelle forced her anger to stay down. "The uncle's name is Phillipi."

Alec frowned. "That's the name Demir gave you?"

"That's what he said."

"That's not Russian."

Janelle let go of the fabric and sighed. "He wasn't talking about Russians. He was talking about his uncle. I thought he was Greek."

"So that's it? That's all he told you?"

"Yes," she said flippantly. "That's it, and apparently all lies. Everything I was told was a lie, I guess. I haven't been a help to you at all. You should have just left me in jail. It probably would have made things a lot easier for you."

"Stop it." His voice was a low growl.

Her own voice had grown higher-pitched and louder, and she was past the point of wanting to stop. "Why should I? I'm sick of being told what to do. I'm sick of people mistrusting me and prying me open for information and interrogating me and accusing me. I'm sick of all of it! I'm sick of you!"

"You're getting hysterical. Lower your voice. Someone will hear."

The fury burst upward from inside her, and she swung her arm hard and hit Alec in the jaw. Stunned at her outburst, he didn't react for several seconds. But when he did, by grasping her wrist, she swung her other hand in a wide arc, slapping at him, trying to claw at him.

He caught her other wrist in his hand and pushed her onto the bed. She landed on her back, still fighting him even after he had thrown himself on top of her. Her very impotence gave her a strength that neither he nor she would have thought her body could contain. He tried to cover her mouth to prevent her from drawing unwanted attention with her screams.

"Shut up, Janelle! Dammit, please!"

She hurled a vicious invective at him and attempted to loosen her fists so as to strike out at him. Not knowing what else to do, Alec covered her mouth with his own. She continued to buck and fight him, but he held her tight, his warm mouth opening over hers and demanding nothing less than her total surrender.

As suddenly as the tirade had begun, it stopped. Alec felt her body subside beneath him like a wave that had washed up on the beach and was then pulled, unprotesting, back to sea.

He tasted her lips beneath his own, warm, salty with tears, quivering. Her whole body began to shake as the sobs racked through her arms and legs and stomach. He shifted his weight, but gathered her up into the fold of his arms, his mouth sliding against her wet cheek and into her hair. "Shh, Janelle, please. I didn't mean to hurt you. I'm sorry."

She cried into the warm depression of his neck and felt the security of his body wrap around her and insulate her from the terror that existed outside the walls of this room.

"Why am I doing this?" she whispered against his skin, then regretted the loosening of his arms. He raised himself up slightly, his weight propped on his elbows. He held her head between his hands.

"If anyone has a right to cry, Janelle, it's you."

She sniffled. "That's not what I meant."

He brushed away a tear on her cheek. "Then what?"

"All of this. I'm so scared. I hate this running and hiding. I ought to just turn myself in and get it over with!"

"Is that what you really want?"

"I want to be a bird, Alec. I want to fly away from all of this. The shadows are everywhere. I see them in my sleep, stalking me, all around me, circling me. I just want to be free of them."

His head dropped down, and his mouth grazed slowly and gently from her temple to her mouth. The touch of his fingers against her scalp spread through her like warm wine. She lifted her arms to his shoulders and felt the pressure of his lips increase with an urgency that had not been there a moment before. She welcomed it, returned it, and allowed it to expand inside her.

A low, warm chuckle came from her throat. "This is getting to be a habit."

His lips followed the arch of her neck down to her collarbone. "What's that?" he breathed against her skin."

"You tackling me and throwing yourself on top of me just to keep me from making an ass of myself. And then me falling to pieces in your arms."

His weight shifted and he lifted higher, his lower body pressed into hers. The movement stole her breath away. His mouth was beside her ear. "You can fall to pieces in my arms anytime."

Her breath quickened at the feather-light touch of his hand as it skimmed along her side, finding her rib cage and lifting up to cover her breast. She wanted to lose herself in the pure warmth of his hands. But even more than that, she wanted to know this man who had become her life-support system and her only link to the world of sanity.

"Who are you, Alec Hayden?" she whispered against his skin, and he raised up enough to look at her. "How can I know your strength and bruising power, yet still be amazed at how gentle you are?"

"Gentle." His scoff was a husky moan that brushed warmly against her face. "If you knew what I'd like to do to you and with you right now."

She held her breath and let it out slowly. Smiling, she shook her head. "You're a strange man, Alec Hayden. You're always so confident, so sure of everything. You try to project that tough-guy image. And yet you really are a gentle man. You also seem to be very much alone."

His breathing evened out, and the line of his mouth became thin and taut. "It's easier that way."

"Not for me."

Absently he watched his thumb stroke a path along her jaw. "I've never taken care of anyone, Janelle. Erin didn't exactly bring out the protective instinct in me. I'm not sure I can do it. I'm not good at sharing myself. The work I do doesn't invite close relationships, and certainly not a lot of honesty."

"Were you lying when you said you worked on security at embassies?"

"No, but that's only part of what I do. I'm sort of a jack-of-all-trades, a troubleshooter. International law is my specialty."

"Is that why James Bluminfeld asked you to help get me released from jail?"

Alec was hesitant to answer. "That wasn't exactly what he asked me to do." He frowned. "I was... interested from the beginning, because of who your father was."

"I see." For some reason, that had never entered her mind. But now that she thought about it, the arrest of a former diplomat's daughter would be of interest to the State Department. "Does Bluminfeld know that you came to Greece to see Nikos?"

"No. No one knows, except you."

"Can you tell me what it is you're after?"

His thumb traced the shape of her lips and then stopped at the corner. "I can't do that, Janelle."

"I see." She sighed beneath him, and he shifted his body. The moment for anything closer was lost. They had both re-erected their defenses. "Should we try to retrieve the coin?"

"Sure." He lifted himself off her and drew her up into a sitting position. Picking up the figurine, he held it in his lap. "Do you have any tweezers in your purse?"

She shook her head. "You can pull the strings off if you want. I liked the little guy, but I'm not sure it's something I want to keep anymore. Just get the coin however you can."

With his fingers, Alec pried loose the strings of the violin, then slipped his hand into the sound hole and pulled out the wedged coin. He flipped it over in his hand, then dropped it into her outstretched palm.

"A gold solidus," she said, turning it over so the face on the front was revealed.

"It's said to be history's most stable currency—held its value for seven centuries."

"That's Constantine in the front." She continued to stare at the coin. "See the jewel in place of his eye? Zafer told me about that. That's what makes this coin so special, because there aren't any others like it. He said that was the way his uncle would know to give him the treasures."

"It's special any way you look at it. Constantine introduced those things in the fourth century."

Janelle turned the coin over and examined the other side. "It must be very valuable."

"To those who want it, it's obviously worth killing for."

She looked at Alec. "You know, I get the feeling that this situation goes way beyond some Russian diplomat. If the State Department was called in, it must have something to do with Americans here. Would I be correct in assuming that the embassy figures into it?"

He hesitated before answering. "That would be a correct assumption."

Janelle watched him closely. "But you don't want me to ask you for more details."

"That's right."

"And you expect me just to sit back and wait in some rural village while you take the coin and go in search of the answers." Her tone was not questioning. She was stating the facts as she saw them.

Alec confirmed them. "Yes. That's exactly what I expect."

Janelle nodded slowly. Her life had somehow gotten away from her. Nothing was within her control anymore. Events happened to her, around her, because of her, but she had no say in them. It was the total lack of control that frightened her the most. Nothing made sense—not her job, not her fleeing from jail, not her feelings toward Alec. She wanted desperately to regain that control.

Janelle placed the coin in Alec's hand and watched him drop it into the left pocket of his jacket. Somehow, she was going to get that control back. She lifted her eyes to his face. "I have been a good girl all my life, Alec. I have done exactly what I was told to do. Look where it got me."

He sat very still and studied her. "I'm listening."

"You can help me get out of Athens," she said. "And you can ship me off to some village to get me out of the way. But I won't stay there in that hotel. Not this time, Alec. This time I'm going to do what I want to do. My life, my freedom and my reputation are at stake here. I intend to get them back.''

''Don't be—'' He had started to say ''stupid,'' but the word wouldn't come out. It just didn't fit her. She was an extremely intelligent woman, and he was not going to pretend she was otherwise. Janelle was different from most of the women he had known. She commanded respect. But what could he tell her that wouldn't put her in even more danger? And how could he convince her to stay in Volos? She was determined to clear her name, and that could only bring her closer to her own murder. Whoever had killed Nikos would not stop there. And Janelle Lindsey might just find herself the next victim.

He couldn't let that happen. He wasn't sure exactly what he felt for her, but he knew it was different from the feelings he'd had for other women. And it was more than just a compelling physical draw. That worried him. He had been alone for too long, trusting no one but himself, finding physical gratification whenever he needed it. He wasn't sure what to do with these absurd notions of wanting to include Janelle in his life and his problems. All he knew was that he didn't want her to get hurt. He didn't want to lose her.

He stood up and removed his jacket, dropping it over the back of a chair, then went across the room to the window. He flicked aside the curtain and stared down at the street. ''I have to see a couple of people here in Athens, and then I'm going to Thessaloniki to meet with Billy Lefland, a friend of mine on the consulate staff there. He's got some information for me that may crack this thing wide open.'' Alec turned around and looked at Janelle. "If I tell you that I'll come to Volos and explain everything to you there, will you stay?"

She grinned. "And behave myself?"

Her smile did nothing to ease the flow of sap that ran strong and full-bodied through him. But with a heroic effort, he smiled back. "Like the good girl you are."

"What if you don't come?"

"I said I would. I just have to take care of a couple of things first. It's my job, Janelle."

Janelle watched him turn his back on her and look down at the street again. This was the moment. She might not have another chance. If she was going to do it, she had to do it now.

Very carefully and quietly, she moved to the chair, slipped her hand into his jacket pocket and removed the coin. She dropped it into the pocket of her dress only seconds before he turned to face her once again. She smiled and walked over to him. She didn't want to deceive Alec any more than she wanted him to deceive her. She wanted to believe that he would continue to help her, but her fear had taken away too many of her convictions.

He was looking down at her, yet she couldn't read what was in his eyes. All she wanted to do was touch him. She wanted to lay her hand against the side of his neck. She wanted to rest her head against the sturdy pillow of his chest. And she wanted him to touch her. But something held her back. "Last night you suggested I should not trust anyone."

Alec wanted to reach out for her and pull her against him. He wanted to throw her on the bed and bury himself inside her. With any other woman, he might have done that. But not with this one. Not with this pretty, vulnerable woman who was standing here talking of trust. He didn't even trust his own feelings at that moment. "That's the best way to survive," he finally said, reminding himself as well as her.

She lifted her hands to the sides of his face, stood on tiptoe and pressed her lips against his. Smiling at his surprise, she whispered, "If there is one thing I intend to be, Alec Hayden, it's a survivor."

Chapter Nine

"Here, let me retie the scarf." Alec's fingers deftly looped the folds of the scarf. "Perfect. I'd never know you."

"Are you sure? I feel like an idiot in this outfit. Especially these shoes—they look like boats."

Alec chuckled. "You'll get used to them. It's the only way, Janelle." The smile faded, and he placed his hands on her shoulders, looking down into her eyes. "I'm too much a part of the embassy team right now. I wouldn't be able to sneak you out. You have to do it this way."

"I know that." The words were weak and her breath got lodged in her throat when his thumb began to stroke against the slim line of skin at her neck that was exposed between blouse and scarf.

"I'm going to show up there, you know." His own voice was low and gentle.

Her eyes closed at the thought of what she had done. Maybe she should tell him. Maybe she should put the coin back. But then...then she would have no guarantees of anything. "I know you are" was all she said, and the words were almost drowned out by the sound of her heart pounding loudly in her chest as his mouth drew near.

He kissed her then and put his arms around her. She wanted to stay in the circle of his arms. She wanted the warmth of his mouth, the taste of his tongue, the pressure of his hand at the base of her spine to go on and on. She didn't want to leave him. There was always the chance that she might not make it, that she would be stopped before she even boarded the bus for Volos.

He drew back and smiled down at her. "Did you take everything you needed from your purse?"

"Yes."

"Passport? Money? Billy Lefland's number in Thessaloniki?"

"Yes, Alec."

He glanced at his watch, and his shoulders sagged. "Okay, it's time. The bus will be pulling up any minute at the corner. Now remember, if I get detained and you need anything, call Billy. He's a good friend. You can trust him."

She nodded, but inside she knew that she could trust only herself and her own ability to survive. That was all she had left. "I'm ready," she said, moving out of his arms. She glanced around the room one last time and walked to the door. "You'll watch from the window?"

He nodded. "Yeah. I'll make sure you get on the bus."

Her heart flipped over as she watched him go over to the chair and pick up his jacket. She didn't even breathe while he slipped it on. Then she opened the door and stepped out into the hall. "Thank you, Alec."

He smiled. "Anytime."

Janelle closed the door and went quickly down the hallway, wondering what he would think when he realized what she had done. Suppose he put his hand in his pocket before she got out of the hotel? Would he try to catch her? Would he chase her down even if it meant exposing her to any police who might be around?

She walked out the front door of the hotel and down the sidewalk toward the bus stop. She glanced up at Alec's window and saw him standing there, smiling. Out of the corner of her eye she noticed a policeman approaching, and a tremor of fear shot through her. She couldn't move. She couldn't make her feet budge from the spot on the sidewalk. She felt a line of perspiration along her neck, beneath the scarf.

The bus rounded the corner and stopped. A crowd of people pressed toward the door. After what seemed an eternity, the policeman walked on by and turned at the next intersection. Janelle glanced again at Alec, who gave her a thumbs-up sign. Swallowing hard over what she was about to do to this man who had taken care of her, she slid her hand into her skirt pocket and took out the coin. As she held it up, the gold glinted in the morning sun. Its brilliance momentarily blinded her, so she couldn't see what Alec's immediate reaction was. But after she put the solidus back in her pocket, Janelle saw that he was no longer smiling. His face was grave, and his eyes were as gray and murky as the leaden sky.

She hurried to the corner and boarded the bus. Within seconds, it pulled away from the curb. She was on her way out of Athens, on her way to even more uncertainty.

FROM THE SEA to the barren ridge of Mount Egaleo, the densely populated seaport of Piraeus mushroomed, spreading its wharves, dockyards, mills, factories and foundries in every direction. Crowded into the main harbor were ships from around the world, each one proudly flying her colors high on the masts. Separated from the center of Athens by six miles of suburbia, Piraeus was the main port and industrial center of Greece.

The two men sat in an open-air café. Their table was near the edge of the port, with a view overlooking the badly polluted water. Frank Osborn dug into his plate of stuffed mussels, while Alec nursed a Fix Hellas beer.

"Sure you won't have some of this?" Frank asked, spearing a bite with his fork. "It's the best in town."

Alec shook his head. "Mussels for breakfast doesn't hold a great deal of appeal for me. And how is it anyway that you always manage to find these little out-of-the-way places?"

"I'm a hound dog, Hayden. You know that. You give me a new town anywhere in the world, and within a week I'll have sniffed out the best meal there. Yessirree, I'm a hound dog, I tell ya."

Somewhere in the distance, a church bell clanged and a ship's horn blew. "Well," Alec mused, sitting back with his beer, "I'm sort of a hound dog myself. But I sniff out information."

Frank glanced up. "I figured this was more than a date. Does this mean we're not going steady?"

Alec laughed. "I'm afraid so."

"Okay, so what's on your mind? Is it the Lindsey case?"

"Partly." God, what an understatement! He had thought of little else ever since he'd watched her climb into the bus that morning. Good girl, hah! He had stared after her, unable to believe that she had actually taken the coin from him. And then to hold it up, to show it to him with that innocent look of hers—that was what really irked him. How on earth had he allowed her to bamboozle him that way? He must definitely be losing his touch. Or else she had cast some spell over him that had turned him into an incompetent boob. He never trusted anyone, so why the hell had he trusted her?

Frank shook his head. "She sure pulled one over on all of us, disappearing the way she did. I didn't expect that from her. I thought she was one of those mild-mannered sorts who always do what they're supposed to. Nope, I just never expected that."

"Neither did I." Alec took a long drink of his beer. "Resourcefulness seems to be a trait that she hides very well, pulling it out at odd little moments." Janelle had changed everything. Messed up all of his plans. Now he had no choice but to go to Volos. She had made sure of that. He finished the beer and ordered another. "The day you called her—when she was released from jail—what was said between you?"

"Seems we've gone over all this before, Alec."

"Indulge me, Frank. I'm just looking for answers, that's all."

Frank licked his fork and took a swig of Retsina wine. "She said somebody named Boris had called her and threatened her about some coin. I told her she was probably mistaken."

"Why?"

"Oh, come on, Alec. You don't believe she was talking about that commie Ivanov over at the Russian embassy...do you?"

"How many other Borises do you know in this town?"

"I'm sure there are plenty. Besides, she was probably just mistaken on the name. I mean, I don't get it. What could Ivanov's involvement possibly be in this, unless... Hey, you think Janelle Lindsey's a spook? KGB maybe?"

Alec wrapped his fingers around the cold bottle of beer. "I think she's a pawn."

Frank continued to play with his fork. "If you know something, old buddy, something that the rest of us should know, maybe you oughta spell it out."

"All I know is that there are a lot of unanswered questions."

"Such as?"

"Such as, what was our good comrade doing at the embassy yesterday?"

"Boris?"

"Yes."

"He and Bluminfeld were holed up in the inner sanctum for several hours. But hell, Hayden, you know I'm not privy to the details. I'm a glorified gatekeeper, nothing more." He shrugged. "I heard they were talking about Mount Athos again, but that's all I know. What is the deal with all those Russian monks up there anyway?"

"The Patriarch of Moscow is in charge of the national churches in the Soviet Union. And I use the term 'church' in the most general sense."

"The immortal shrine of Marx," Frank said.

"Yes, but Russia still sends monks to Mount Athos. The catch—and the reason we're so interested—is that once those monks move into the monasteries, they automatically become Greek citizens."

"An insidious plot to take over the Mediterranean, no doubt."

Alec laughed. "Maybe. Maybe not. The point is, we want to stay in tune."

"And that falls under Bluminfeld's territory?"

"Yes."

"Okay," Frank said, digging into the mussels again, "but I still don't see what that has to do with Janelle Lindsey and the murder of Nikos what's-his-name."

"Neither do I, Frank. But nevertheless, a connection is there. Janelle was almost run over at the airport by someone driving a car from the Russian embassy. She was threatened by a man named Boris. Zafer Demir mentioned Boris Ivanov to her. He also talked about Mount Athos. The connection is definitely there."

"So you think someone with our embassy is involved also."

"Yes."

Frank set the fork down and leaned back in his chair. "Am I a suspect?"

"Not anymore."

Frank nodded slowly, digesting that bit of information in his own thoughtful way. "Okay," he said, "so what can I do to help?"

"I'm going to Thessaloniki to meet with Billy Lefland. I think he'll be able to give us some help."

"He should. He's a hound dog, too. Looks like some sort of damn hippie, but he's good. So what do ya need me for?"

"Is anyone at the embassy working with the Greek Ministry of Antiquities? Any ongoing projects with some of the digs?"

"There are always Americans looking for permission to excavate, professors mostly. Nothing that I would call sinister."

"Have you heard anyone talk about Vasilos Voutsas, the minister over there at Antiquities? Has his name been bounced around?"

"I've heard it mentioned a few times but..." Frank shrugged. "Nothing in particular."

"How about a man named Mavro Sklavopoulos?"

"No—but wait a minute. I've been going over the phone tapes of the past week, trying to catch up. There *was* a call from Antiquities. It went through Bluminfeld's office. Janelle Lindsey took the call."

Alec didn't move. "What was discussed?"

"Nothing much, that I can recall. At least when I listened to the tape, I didn't find anything out of the ordinary."

"Will you check it again?"

"Sure."

"This morning?"

"Okay, Alec. You can go over the tapes with me, for that matter. You know, this thing with the girl has got everybody tied up in knots. It's all over the political community, and Bluminfeld's like a wet hornet. The local gendarmerie, as well as the police all over Attica, are looking for her. I tell you, even if Lindsey's cleared of the charges, her career is dead and gone."

"I think you underestimate her."

"Maybe so. You've talked to her more than the rest of us have. I don't suppose you know where she might have gone?"

The question was innocent enough, but Alec's gaze narrowed on Frank's face. "No. Do you?"

"Hell no, boy. I don't know didly squat. But I'll tell ya, if I were putting my money on this thing with the embassy, I'd be mighty tempted to put it on Dimitris."

"Why?"

"I don't know. I don't trust that guy. I never have. Of course, if truth be known, I don't trust Lindsey or Bluminfeld or you or—"

Alec chuckled. "I thought you didn't trust anyone who wasn't a native-born American."

"Wrong, Hayden. I don't trust anybody who isn't a native-born Texan."

"So tell me about Dimitris. Is he a coke user?"

"Probably. But Bluminfeld likes him, so everybody just looks the other way. Hell, I don't know. Maybe they've got something going on the side."

"Does Dimitris deal with Antiquities?"

"I suppose. He's in on everything. Is that what all this is about, then? Has one of the archaeological digs uncovered something?"

"No." Alec sat back and drained his beer, saying nothing more.

Frank shook his head. "You State Department types are all alike—love to keep the rest of us guessing."

"Makes life more interesting that way."

Frank snorted. "Well, all I care about is that I'm not on your list of suspected swindlers, frauds, murderers, thieves, rapists or whatever else you have in mind. In fact, I'd say that damn near calls for another drink. How 'bout it, Hayden? Are you buying this round or am I?"

"I tell you what, Frank. You get me those phone tapes, and I'll buy you all the Retsina you can drink."

"That, my boy, is my kind of deal."

THE TRAIN ENGINE spewed diesel fuel into the already thick, gray air. Crudely built crates were loaded onto the broad shoulders of men stained with sweat and fatigue. They didn't care what was in the crates or where the cargo was going. They simply unloaded them into the rail cars, filled in their hours, punched the time card and went home at the end of the day.

But two of the men standing in the middle of the train yard did care what was in the crates. They knew exactly where the cargo was going. It would travel through Lamia, bypassing Volos, then go through Larisa and on to Kalambaka. They knew what time it would arrive at the monastery in Meteora. Sometime soon—a week, a month, whenever Ivanov gave the word—the crates of gold and bronze and silver icons would be transported to Mount Athos. From there, it was only a matter of which country to route them through. Perhaps through Bulgaria, perhaps Yugoslavia, perhaps even Turkey. At that point, the treasures would be home free. They would arrive, one way or another, at the Saint Sophia Cathedral in Kiev.

VOLOS WAS AN INDUSTRIAL TOWN, choked with ferry traffic. Very little remained of its ancient history. But above the city proper, cypress-clad hills overlooked the town and the calm waters of the gulf. The green slopes of Mount Pilio were dotted with colorful villages. Clear, bubbling mountain streams rushed through the beech, chestnut and olive groves on their way to the sea.

The bus had let Janelle off at the edge of the town near a deep ravine that separated Volos from the village of Makrinitsa. From there she had walked to the hotel and was given a small clean room. She knew beyond a shadow of a doubt that Alec would come to Volos. She put her hand into the deep pocket of the gray skirt and smiled. Her guarantee was right there. He wanted the coin, therefore he would come to Volos. Janelle was sure he wouldn't waste any time in getting here, either. And then she would have another opportunity to find out what was going on. There was no way she would hang around this village on the slim chance that he might show up for her one of these days. No, it was time for her to start calling some of the shots on her own.

Every time she thought of the look on his face when the bus had pulled away, she couldn't help but smile. Tough, dominant Alec Hayden, who thought no one was as capable at this game as he was.

How many times had he played games like this before? What had he done for the State Department all these years? International law, he had said. But what exactly did that mean? That term could apply to anything from reading contracts to tracking down terrorists.

Alec claimed that his wife had enjoyed his trips away from home too much. How much of the time had he been gone? What dark secrets had she known or suspected about him? Or had it all been her fault? Janelle had seen enough in her parents' life together to know that it took two to make or break a marriage. But how could anyone be unfaithful to Alec Hayden? Just the thought of being with him, touching him, lying with him, filled Janelle with the most compelling urges she had ever known. With Nikos, she'd been tempted by the idea of doing something her parents would never have approved of. With Alec, it was a need that went beyond the physical. He had taken over something within her, and she wondered if she would ever be free of it even if and when he disappeared from her life, which was one thing she felt reasonably sure he would do.

Once the situation was resolved—if it ever could be—she knew he would go on with his life as planned. He had a good career. He was needed. He had commitments. And she? What would happen to Janelle Lindsey when all this was over? She couldn't imagine going back to Athens and picking up where she had left off—let alone working with the very man who had believed her guilty of murder. James Bluminfeld had turned against her. She could never work with him again.

But where would she go? What would she do? Maybe she would be reassigned to another embassy. Maybe she would be let go.

Janelle sat on the edge of the bed in her hotel room and sighed. Her whole future was out of her control. Well, almost.

Her hand closed over the coin in her pocket and she smiled once again. Even Alec had taken over her life. But although he might have control of her emotions, right now she had control over his actions. And if that did not place them on equal footing, at least it was Janelle's first step in regaining control over her own destiny.

THE HIGHWAY WAS A PAVED ROAD that cut a clean path through the plains, where Spartans had made a heroic stand against Xerxe's army in the fifth century B.C. Soon, the road curved back to the coast, to rim the narrow sea. The countryside lay warm and sleepy under the afternoon sun, with olive groves sloping down into valleys.

Alec saw little of it from his rental car. He was intent on only one thing—reaching Volos, getting the coin from Janelle and heading for Mount Athos. After studying the phone tapes Frank had provided and talking over his theories with Vasilos Voutsas at the Ministry of Antiquities, he now knew what he was looking for. The only thing he didn't know was where the coin fitted in. Who wanted it? And why?

But Janelle had it now, and he was going to get it. Then he would let Boris know he had it. Once he did that, things would start happening. Until then, he had only theory and speculation to go on.

An image of Janelle—flashing that bright coin from the sidewalk below his hotel window—came to his mind. Angered, he slapped the steering wheel, undecided about what to do with her when he reached Volos. His first impulse was to vent his anger on her, but the signal kept getting crossed with his desire to kiss her and hold her. He could not let go of that crazy dream. Actually, it should be so simple to deal with her. But it wasn't. She had twisted him around inside, complicating the whole picture, to say nothing of what she had done to his nights. Logically, he knew that he could get the coin. She was a woman who, by her own admission, had limited experience. If Nikos Marinatos could have duped her, then he, Alec Hayden, certainly could. But did he want to? That was the question that continually plagued him. She wasn't like Erin. She wasn't like any other woman in his experience. So he didn't know what to do with her. If he was the man he thought he was, he'd get the coin by whatever means it took and be on his way. That was what he would do if...

BY MIDAFTERNOON, the four walls of her room began to close in on her. Janelle left the hotel and walked into the square, looking for a place to have lunch. The square was a large paved terrace that overhung the town and the gulf below. A man, seated in a hard chair in one corner, spun clay pots. In another corner, three men clustered around a table and played backgammon.

After buying a lemonade and a spiced sausage, Janelle sat down against the cool whitewashed wall of a Byzantine chapel. Because it was afternoon, most of the shops were boarded up for siesta. Even the man with the clay pots and the men playing backgammon soon picked up their chairs and went home for a nap. Only an old man, dragging a mule and a load of grapes, still lumbered by. All else was now quiet.

The sun slid lower. A bird circled lazily overhead. A woman gathered in her laundry from a balcony. Another closed the shutters on her windows. Time drifted by on a slow, rhythmic note.

It felt good to float and to let the world meander around her. Janelle had seldom done this. She had always been on the move. There had been so little time for reflection, so little time to stop at the crossroads and think about which path she wanted to take. Her life had been a nonstop climb to the top, always striving to reach the pinnacle, where her father was. When she received the coveted post in Athens, she felt that she had made it at least halfway to the top. But now,

the life she had planned and worked for lay in a battered heap at the bottom of the hill. As soon as she was
cleared of the criminal charge—if she ever was
cleared—she would have to start all over from scratch.
The idea made her uncommonly weary. She wasn't at
all sure she had it in her to begin again.

She closed her eyes and breathed deeply. For now,
she was not going to think. She was going to float. . . .
The afternoon faded toward sunset. The air wafted
over her face and neck. She felt cool all over.

"You had to do it, didn't you?"

With her hand shading her eyes, Janelle looked up
into Alec's face. He was standing over her, his hands
thrust into the pockets of his jeans. His expression was
unreadable, his mouth a straight line.

"You just had to do it," he repeated.

"Yes," she answered. "I had to do it."

"I told you I would come for you."

"I had no guarantee of when."

He stooped down beside her, and she saw that the
anger had not left his face. "What guarantees do you
have now?"

Even angry, he looked good to her—strong, so
masculine, so sure of himself. Her hand left the fold
of her skirt and lifted to his jaw. His skin was cool
against the warmth of her palm. "Only that you are
here. That was all the guarantee I wanted."

He tried to ignore the heat from her hand, tried to
pretend that it meant nothing to him. "Where is it?"
he asked, but was aware of an acute disappointment
when her hand dropped back to her side.

"In my room," she answered solemnly. What had
she expected? She had known that he would be angry.

She hadn't really expected him to come in and sweep her into his arms . . . had she?

"I came to get the coin, Janelle."

Listening carefully to his tone, she was positive he was trying to convince himself of that fact as much as he was trying to convince her. "Okay," she said. "Let's go."

Together they crossed the quiet courtyard. A couple of shopkeepers had returned and were rearranging their wares on the shelves. A solitary player sat at a corner table and shuffled his deck of cards, waiting for an opponent.

The hotel was small and Spartan, but very clean. They climbed the steps to the second floor and walked down the narrow hallway to her room. Once inside, Janelle went over to the bureau and opened the top drawer. From between the folds of a sheet of paper, she withdrew the coin, then closed her fingers around it. She looked at Alec. He was standing perfectly still just inside the closed door.

If she gave it to him, he would go. Nothing would be changed. He would head off to find the truth, and she would be stuck here with only a memory full of lies to keep her company. She moved toward him. "I'm not some casual bystander, Alec. Much of what has happened has happened to me."

He was quiet for so long, his eyes boring relentlessly into hers, that she thought she would go crazy. "Say something . . . please."

He opened his mouth to speak, but the only thing that came out was a resigned sigh. Then, slowly, he untied the scarf she was wearing and removed it, brushing a loose dark strand away from her face. "I could...I should just take it, you know, and be on my way."

Her eyes never left his face. "Yes, I know."

The back of his hand stroked her cheek and his fingers trailed down the side of her neck, over her collarbone, down the front of her sweater. "Why are you doing this to me, Janelle?"

She swallowed hard, suddenly in need of breath. The touch of his fingers and the intensity of his stare had stolen the air from her lungs. "Doing what?" she finally managed to ask.

"Why do you make me want you so?"

His finger was drawing lazy circles around her breast. All she wanted to do was to close her eyes and melt against him. Instead, she lifted her chin a fraction and forced herself to look him straight in the eye. "Because you and I are in this together, Alec." He was watching the movements of his finger and said nothing, so she continued. "Did you know that in some cultures, if a man saves someone's life, he is stuck with that person forever?"

His finger stopped moving and his hand closed over her breast. With his other arm, he reached around her and pulled her to him. "I do want you, Janelle, but...do you have any idea how much?" His mouth was against her temple, his whisper harsh and reluctant. "Do you have any idea how I fantasize about you—the things I think about...."

His mouth over hers was warm and insistent. Janelle felt her pulse thundering in her ears. "Yes," she said with a sigh when his lips grazed a path down her throat. "Yes," she whispered again. He lifted her in his arms and carried her to the bed.

She was liquid fire throughout her body. Everywhere his fingers touched her, every place where his body met hers, the heat spread over her skin. There was an urgency in his touch, a need to quench the fire that was out of control in his own body.

"What am I going to do with you, Janelle?" he murmured thickly against her throat. But before she could answer, his lips covered hers again. She parted her mouth, offering him everything, answering him with her body.

His fingers worked at the buttons on her sweater, then on her skirt, until she was completely naked. The urgency intensified. His hands and tongue devoured her flesh, and she felt as if she were covered with a thousand tiny needles of pleasure-pain.

She helped him take off his clothes, and then they lay together, their skin touching, their arms wrapped around each other. Neither of them moved. It was enough in this moment that they were sharing each other's warmth, that they were giving each other the peace and comfort they both needed.

But after a while, the urgency returned. Alec's hand slid and found the center of her body. No longer were they content to lie quietly in each other's arms. Now they both wanted more. Janelle wanted everything that Alec could give her. She opened herself to him and knew a completeness she had never known before. He took from her, yes. But he also gave her a sense of herself that had been robbed from her. She had never understood what true giving between a man and a woman could be like, not until today. They worshiped each other's bodies until their mouths and flesh and souls became one in sheer ecstasy.

The window was open to the early evening, and a warm breeze drifted over their bodies. Alec's leg was entwined with hers. He propped himself up on one elbow, studying her face as his finger traced its outlines. "I've always thought of myself as a levelheaded man," he said softly, smiling. "Clear-sighted. But now...now I can't get you out of my mind. You've been with me every minute, night and day."

Janelle smiled up at him and smoothed her hand over his bewildered brow. "It was more than just the information, wasn't it, Alec...more than the coin...the reason you've done all those things for me? The reason we just shared what we did?"

His head bent down and his mouth brushed across her forehead. His answer was a low, hoarse groan. "Yes. It was more than the information, and more than the coin. Until today I didn't want it to be, but it is."

She wrapped her arms around his back and smiled. "I can help you, Alec. Really I can. Despite this mess I'm in, I'm not a total buffoon."

He kissed the tip of her nose. "You've proved that, my love. But the danger is only just beginning. You have to understand that, Janelle. Once they know for sure that we have the coin, they'll come after us."

"How will they know?"

"I'll tell them. It's the only way to expose this thing."

"Don't you think it's high time you told me what this 'thing' is and who 'they' are?"

Alec took a deep breath and lifted his eyes toward the window. The sun was low in the sky and cast a warm orange glow across the room, stretching in a band up over the bed and onto Janelle's body.

"Smuggling," he said after a long pause. His hand was resting on her stomach, and his fingers automatically began a long, slow caress.

"Smuggling of what?"

"Byzantine relics. I've met with the minister of antiquities a couple of times. He's working on this with me, although he doesn't yet know the extent of the embassy's involvement. He suspects, I think, but he doesn't know for sure."

"And do you?"

"No."

Janelle frowned at his chest and lifted her hand to the side of his neck. "But then how do you know—how did you get involved in this?"

"I'm involved because someone at the embassy is involved."

"Who?"

"I'm not sure. I thought for a while it was Frank, but it's not him."

"You told me you came to Greece to meet Nikos. How did you know him?"

"I didn't. He contacted someone at the Ministry of Antiquities who, in turn, contacted the State Department. Apparently Nikos was involved in the smuggling operation and wanted out. He wanted to name names."

"Names of people in our embassy?"

"Yes. And with the Antiquities Department. Mavro Sklavopoulos was one of the people involved. Does that name ring a bell?"

She frowned and shook her head. "I don't know. I don't think so. Oh, this is all so awfully hard to believe." Her eyes closed as the memories washed through her. "How could I not have known that about

Nikos? I mean, I knew there was something wrong with him, but I had no idea that—that it was anything like this." She sighed. "And someone with the embassy..."

He stared down at her closed eyes, then dropped a kiss over each one. "It fits, Janelle. You've said yourself that Nikos quizzed you thoroughly about your job and the people you would work with. Did you ever think that maybe you were being framed for Nikos's murder by someone who knew you? Someone who wanted his or her own involvement covered up?"

"I thought a man named Boris killed Nikos. I never thought of anyone else." She'd opened her eyes and was staring at him.

"What makes you think it was Boris?"

"I guess it was because of things that Zafer said. But then, he wasn't exactly truthful, was he?"

"Not exactly."

"But who at the embassy would do such a thing? I know that Frank turned me in for leaving Athens, but..."

"No, as I said, Frank isn't involved. In fact, he and his taping of telephone conversations helped me to confirm that Sklavopoulos was the person involved over at Antiquities. There was a series of calls from him. He's in charge of all Byzantine relics at the ministry."

"Who took the calls?"

"You took one."

Her eyes widened. "And you think—"

"You switched the call over to Bluminfeld."

She released the breath she was holding. "That's why the name didn't ring a bell, I guess. And—did Bluminfeld take the rest of the calls?"

"Yes."

Janelle stared at Alec, probing for the thoughts beneath his words. "What was discussed?"

"Nothing incriminating."

"Can't this Sklavopoulos fellow be confronted?"

Alec shook his head. "Not right now. He's vacationing in Meteora. Voutsas, the minister over at Antiquities, has tried to contact him, but so far with no luck."

Janelle turned her head toward the window. She could hear laughter in the courtyard below and the sounds of someone singing. "Okay," she said, looking back at Alec. "But if Boris didn't kill Nikos, then what is his connection to all of this?"

"I'm not saying positively that he didn't kill him. I'm just saying that there may be others involved. Someone else could have pulled the trigger. Boris Ivanov is a Russian diplomat. He works directly for the Soviet Secretariat of the Patriarch of Moscow, overseeing all religious activities in Russia. And if that sounds as if he must be as bored as the Maytag repairman, he's a lot busier than you'd think."

"Yes, I know. I went with my father on a diplomatic mission there once. A number of churches are still in operation—actually, 'tolerated' is more like it." She smiled. "Oh, by the way, if we need it, I speak Russian."

His eyes grew dark and cloudy, and his fingers curled against the skin of her stomach. His mouth was stretched thin and tight. "Let's hope like hell you don't have to use it. If anything happened to you, Janelle . . .''

He didn't complete the sentence, but she thought she understood. ''I know,'' she said softly, and laid her hand over his, stroking his fingers to make them relax. ''I couldn't agree more, Alec. That brush with the Russian embassy car is as close as I want to get to Moscow.'' She smiled again to reassure him that she wasn't afraid. It was a lie, but he was worried about enough things already. He didn't need to be worried about her safety, too. ''So finish telling me about Boris.''

''Well, he's in charge of the Russian monks who are sent to Greece to live on Mount Athos.''

''That's in Macedonia, isn't it?''

''Yes, on the Halkidiki peninsula. It's the center of Byzantine monasticism and the Eastern Orthodox religion.''

''And Zafer said that his uncle—or whoever it really is—lives at the Karoulia monastery.''

''Which is on Mount Athos.''

''So then a monk is Boris's contact there?''

''Most likely. He probably hides the relics until they can be shipped out of the country.''

''But why would the Russians want these Christian antiquities?''

''The have-nots always want what they don't have, especially if it's valuable.''

Janelle closed her eyes and let the memory of their lovemaking wash through her. She had wanted the feelings to go on and on. ''I suppose it should all make sense to me, but it just doesn't.''

Alec lazily twirled a strand of her hair with his fingertips. "You're not alone, Janelle. There are too many missing pieces."

At the slight tug of her hair between his fingers, she thought it would be so nice if they could forget about Boris Ivanov and the embassy and the stolen relics for a little while, if they could just concentrate only on themselves and what they meant to each other. But if there was something lasting between them, something aside from her dependency on him and his sense of responsibility toward her, something other than their overwhelming physical draw for each other, it would have to wait until later to be explored.

She sighed and opened her eyes, forcing herself to face the real world. "Okay, Alec, say Boris and Zafer and whoever it is at the embassy are involved in the smuggling, and suppose some monk in a secluded monastery plays a part in storing or transporting or safeguarding the smuggled items...." She stopped and frowned. "What was Nikos's part? Why was he killed?"

Alec's eyes skimmed over her body. His hand moved in concert with his gaze. But after a moment, the wandering of his fingers ceased, and he resigned himself to face the harsher reality that surrounded them. "Assume Nikos wanted out. So he turns to the U.S. government. But he's killed before he can tell us much of anything. You're framed for the murder, the case is wrapped up quickly—no doubt you killed him in a fit of jealous rage or something. That would probably have been the end of the story. We would have had no other leads, except that Nikos didn't have the coin, which is obviously what the killer and his cohorts were after in the first place. They couldn't stop until they had it. So they had to come after you.''

''But why was Nikos at my house? Do you think he had come there for the coin?''

''Probably. He was supposed to meet with me that afternoon, so maybe he was going to give it to me, I don't know. He must not have known that you had the figurine in your office.''

Janelle shook her head sadly. ''No, he didn't. I had taken it there only the day before.'' As she slid her hand slowly up Alec's forearm, she felt a sudden chill and shivered slightly.

Alec reached over for the corner of the bedspread and pulled it up over her. ''Better?''

She smiled gratefully and nodded, but her mind was still on Nikos's death. ''But why would he leave the note telling me to give the coin to Zafer?''

Alec shook his head. ''I don't know, Janelle. That's what puzzles me about it. Maybe he and Zafer were planning on going to the authorities together. But—you do know where the note was found, don't you?''

''In my bedroom, you said.''

Alec hesitated while he studied her face. She had been through so much in only a few short days. Did she have a breaking point? She wanted to know what was going on, and she deserved to know. But how much knowledge was too much? He turned his gaze away from her. ''It was clutched in his hand when he died.'' The blood drained from her face as if through a sieve. Janelle was afraid she might faint, but she didn't want Alec to know that. She covered her eyes with her hands, trying to block out the images that kept assaulting her mind. But they wouldn't go away. The note she had held in her own hands had been forced from a dead man's fingers. From Nikos's fingers. "Oh, God," she whispered in anguish. "I had no idea."

Alec grasped her hands and lifted them to his lips, kissing them. "I'm sorry, Janelle. Maybe it would have been better if..."

Janelle pulled her hands away and reached over to the bedside table for the coin. She held it up, staring at it, turning it over and over between her fingers. Then she cleared her throat and worked hard to speak in a rational, unemotional tone of voice. "So the killer and—and the rest of this gang of thieves are convinced that I have the coin."

Alec nodded. "At least until I can let them know I have it. I want to go to Thessaloniki to see Billy Lefland. He's with the American Consulate there, and he'll be the one to let them know I've got it."

"Do you think what Zafer told me about showing it to the monk is true, or do you think it's some sort of payment for someone's part in this?"

"Payment, probably. But it could be as Zafer said. If this contact at the Karoulia monastery is a real monk and if he's innocent of what is actually going on, then maybe it *is* necessary to show the coin to him. Maybe the coin signifies something special to him, I don't know. I hope that's what we'll find out."

Alec shifted on his elbow and continued to watch Janelle as she examined the coin in her hand. He hoped like hell he was doing the right thing with her. He prayed that he wouldn't push her farther than she could go. He wanted to take the solidus from her hand and draw her close to him. He wanted to make love to her again and again. He realized now that he had made a tremendous commitment to this woman. A commitment to protect her against all pain and hurt. If she insisted on involving herself in this case any further, he might not be able to do that. And that scared the hell out of him.

"Now...now that you know the whole picture, Janelle, do you still want to go on?"

She looked up at him, but said nothing.

He wanted her to realize how dangerous it could be. He didn't want her to make a mistake that would bring her pain. "It will mean placing ourselves right in the middle of it. You realize that, don't you?"

"Yes, I realize that."

He waited for her to say something more, but she didn't. "Well?" he finally asked. "What do you want to do?"

She let her fingers weave through the strands of his thick brown hair. She was warm beneath the blanket, and the breeze from the window felt good on her face. Her voice, when she finally spoke, was soft and wistful. "I want to lie on a beach somewhere, Alec. I want to lie perfectly still and melt beneath the sun. Then I wouldn't have to face any of this." She laid a finger against the corner of his mouth. "That's not the answer you were looking for, is it?"

"You could wait here, Janelle."

She shook her head. "No, I couldn't. Regardless of whether either of us wants it to be this way or not, I— I think you're stuck with me, Alec."

He shifted his body over hers and framed her head with the palms of his hands. When he lowered his mouth to hers, his breath was uneven and warm, his voice low and husky. "I think I am at that."

AN HOUR LATER they were in a small shop in the center of the village square. The clothes Janelle found there weren't the latest fashion, but they fitted her perfectly: beige skirt, a print blouse and a green cardigan sweater. After paying for them, she wore them out of the store and carried her peasant outfit in the shopping bag.

"Want some dinner?" Alec asked.

She laughed. "It seems like with you I'm always hungry. But yes, I do want some food. You know any good places?"

"Where is Frank when you need him?" Alec murmured before setting off to find the local favorite.

They ended up at a place called Eden, where the tables were all set in a rooftop garden. They ordered roast pork, pasta and a bottle of Kokkineli wine.

Alec reached across the table for her hand. "Do you have any idea how upset I was with you when I saw that coin in your hand this morning?"

Janelle took a sip of her wine. "I can well imagine. But at the time it seemed my only choice."

"Despite what I feel for you...and despite what we just shared together, I wish I was convinced that you made the right choice."

"So do I. But I...well, I'm trying to make some decisions for myself. I never have, you know. Everything I've ever done has been programmed by someone else. Every step I took was overseen by my parents. I never even had a chance to fall down. I had no idea how to pick myself up and keep going...until now. And I'm not so sure I won't stumble again."

His fingers wove through hers, and his eyes swept over her face. "You will stumble, Janelle. Lots of times. But you'll get up and try again. As you said, you plan to be a survivor. And I have no doubt you'll succeed.''

Her thumb slid gently over his. ''And what about you, Alec? When this is all over, I suppose you'll just...'' She couldn't find the right words to ask what she wanted to know, so the question drifted away on the cool evening breeze scented with the fragrance of flowers.

Alec's hand moved to his glass of wine. ''I've been alone for a long time, Janelle. It's worked well for me. I travel extensively. I live out of a suitcase half the time and leave on a moment's notice. Some of the things I'm involved in are dangerous. It's been easier that way—being alone.''

''Easier,'' she repeated, watching him closely. ''What about lonelier?''

He took a hefty drink of wine, then met her eyes. ''Sometimes.''

Janelle studied his handsome face for a long moment, her mind filled with wonderment at the feelings she had for him. This afternoon had changed everything for her. Lonely? Yes, she too had been lonely. All her life.

She smiled at him and said softly, ''I know, Alec. Sometimes for me, too.''

Chapter Ten

The Aegean, midnight blue at this late hour, butted and slammed against the Thessaloniki seawall. *Volta*, the traditional evening stroll, was still in full swing, although most of those left in the sidewalk cafés and bars were late-night revelers in search of a party. Alec and Janelle sat side by side at a small, wrought-iron table at Korona, the café named for the white Macedonian wine it served. They had already shared a full bottle between them, and as soon as Billy Lefland arrived, they would no doubt polish off another.

Alec rested his elbows on the table and leaned close to her. "Lefty will be here in less than five minutes. He's always on time."

Janelle took a sip of wine and smiled over the rim of the glass. "You sound disappointed."

He shrugged. "Just rushed, I guess. You brought up something this afternoon in Volos that I'd—well, I'd like to clear it up."

Janelle set her glass down with a sigh. "I was sort of enjoying the respite from this smuggling business. But if we need to talk about—"

"It's not about the case. It's about you."

Her eyes caught with his. She wasn't sure how far she wanted him to probe into her life again, at least not until she felt that she had it back in one piece. "What about me?" she asked reluctantly.

"You said you wanted to go off, to a beach somewhere. You wanted to melt away, forget everything, not face any of it anymore."

"Is that so surprising, Alec? I've had quite a few shocks in the past week. A little rest would—"

"Was it just this past week?"

Janelle picked up her glass and took a drink, stalling for time. She didn't like the direction the conversation had suddenly taken. She wasn't prepared for it. "What do you mean?" she asked, staring into her glass of wine.

"Is it just the past week that you don't want to face anymore, or is it your whole life? I'm not trying to pry into someplace where I'm not welcome, Janelle. I'm simply concerned. From things you've said, it seems that you've been pushed all your life to be someone and something that—that maybe you're not."

She turned her head and watched a young couple stroll arm in arm down the sidewalk. "I passed the foreign service exam, Alec. I did well in the interviews and . . ."

He laid an arm across the back of her chair and, with his other hand, turned her toward him again. "I'm not talking about your qualifications, Janelle. You're a bright woman. Your file told me that. They couldn't have picked a better candidate for the Athens position. But that's not what I'm talking about."

She lowered her gaze to the slim space between their chairs. "I know, Alec. I'm just not sure I know the answer, or even how I feel. I've worked toward this all my life. I think it'd be very difficult for me if I found out I don't even want it."

With his hand on the back of her head, he pulled her close and sought her lips. The warmth from his fingers, tangled in the length of her hair, spread through her body like that of a fine cognac. His mouth trailed leisurely to her ear, and his voice became a low murmur. "When this is all over, let's go to that beach—wherever you have in mind—and melt together under the sun."

A feverish shiver raced over her, tingling every nerve ending, as his mouth slipped down to the side of her neck. "Will it ever be over, Alec? Will we ever be free of it?"

"Yes," he whispered. "I promise it will be over soon. And I'll take you to that beach. You won't have to think about anything. I'll take care of you."

Her head fell back against his hand, and she closed her eyes. "It sounds like heaven."

"I hate to have to bring you two back down to earth," a loud voice boomed. "But we got business here."

Janelle jumped back in her chair and stared up into a huge nest of hair. Two squinty eyes, a bulbous nose and a wicked grin poked out from behind the mass of red beard and sideburns and flyaway mane.

Alec laughed and relaxed, still resting his arm along the back of Janelle's chair. "Janelle, meet Lefty Lefland, known as William T. Lefland, Jr. to his closest friends."

Janelle stuck out her hand, and Billy looked at it as if he'd never seen a female hand before. "Hi," he said in a gruff voice, then plopped down in the vacant chair. Janelle brought her untouched hand back to her lap.

Alec leaned toward Janelle's ear, but spoke loud enough for Billy to hear. "Lefty's scared to death of girls."

Billy's laugh bounded off the surrounding tables. A Greek waiter walked by, and Billy ordered a beer. "Now," he said, turning to Alec and Janelle with a look of ferocious intent, "looks like we got us a dead skunk in our midst. And where I come from in South Dakota, dead skunks'll stink up the air for miles around."

"Did you check on those shipments?" Alec asked.

"Yep. After you called yesterday, I checked every manifest I could get my hands on from the various shipping companies. There have been a series of cargo transfers in the past few months—not all by ship. Some were by train, some by truck. But they all went to the same place."

"Athos?" Janelle asked.

"Meteora. The latest shipment was a week ago."

Her confused expression was identical to Alec's. "Meteora?"

"Yep. And a month ago, there was one from Meteora to Athos."

Alec poured more wine into their glasses. "So Meteora is used as a halfway house, maybe. And when there is enough cargo, it goes to Athos."

"Looks that way," Billy said, slamming his bottle of beer to the table. The waiter was there immediately to ask if he would like another. "Hell, no," he boomed. "I only took one sip."

"What is in Meteora?" Janelle asked, trying not to laugh at his bizarre behavior.

"Monasteries," Billy answered.

"Just like in Athos?"

"No. Mostly just ruins. There may be one or two still operating. I'm not sure."

Janelle turned to Alec. "Didn't you say that Mavro Sklavopoulos was vacationing there?"

"Yes." To Billy, he said, "Sklavopoulos is in charge of Byzantine relics for the Ministry of Antiquities."

Billy took a huge swig of his beer. "Well, I'll be damned. Guess I'd better check on where he might be staying."

"That would help," Alec agreed. "His boss has been unable to locate him so far, but you may have better luck. So," he added, "we know now that the shipments go to Meteora first and then to Athos."

"Yeah," said Billy. "I also found out that another shipment went from Athos to Yugoslavia about two weeks ago."

Janelle frowned. "But if that shipment contained the smuggled artifacts, then we must be too late. They've already been sent out of the country!"

"Unless that's only part of it," Alec said. "It's probably an ongoing operation."

Janelle turned to Billy. "Do all of the shipments originate from Athens?"

"No, but the orders are processed there. And this is where it begins to stink. All the shipments were labeled as property of the American government and cleared by the embassy in Athens."

"Our embassy?" Janelle gasped.

Billy nodded. "Ours. And the orders had the shipping-department stamp on them. It would have made no sense at all, except that Alec called me yesterday and told me what he was looking into."

"Was there any name at all on the last order?" Alec asked. "The one that went out a week ago?"

"No, just the standard U.S. seal."

Alec turned to Janelle. "Who's in charge of shipping there?"

She frowned, trying to remember. "I think Dimitris has been in charge of that department."

"Nope," Billy said, shaking his head at Alec. "When you told me to check up on Dimitris, I tried to find a connection between him and the shipping orders. There simply isn't any. In fact, on the date of the last order, he was out of town."

"Then who stamped the order?" Alec growled.

Janelle sat motionless, frowning down at the table. When she spoke, her voice was soft and tentative. "If Dimitris was gone that week, then everything would have been handled through Bluminfeld's office." She looked up and stared into Alec's gray eyes. He was very still. "I had nothing to do with it, Alec. I mean, I worked for Bluminfeld, and that was something that would fall under my duties, but . . ."

Alec hesitated, then reached over and laid his hand on her arm. "I'm not accusing you of anything."

"Your eyes say more than you think."

His gaze veered away. "I'm simply looking for answers, Janelle. Just as you are."

Billy sensed the tension rising between the two across the table. "Looks like my exit cue," he said, shoving back his chair and rising. "I suggest, Alec, that you get down to Meteora and see what in hell is going on."

Alec was watching Janelle, but she wouldn't look at him. Her mouth was thin and tight, and her eyes were directed on the center of the table. He looked up at

Billy. "That's exactly where I'm going, Lefty. But I need you to do me a favor. Call Vasilos Voutsas and update him. He's the Greek minister of antiquities. I've been keeping him informed, but he needs to hear about the shipments to Meteora. Tell him we're heading there now. Fill him in on everything. And tell him to send reinforcements."

Billy drained the last of his beer while standing and slammed the bottle back to the table. "I'll see if I can get hold of him tonight."

"Good. I appreciate your help."

"Yeah, well, you owe me one, Hayden. See ya. Nice meeting you, Janelle."

She finally looked up. "Yes, you too."

Without another word, Billy turned and strode off, disappearing in a crowd of merrymakers that were making a human chain across the sidewalk. Janelle took a drink of her wine, still refusing to look at Alec. Then she put the glass down, stood up and walked quickly away from the table, heading in the opposite direction from which Billy had taken.

Alec wasted no time in catching up to her. Grasping her arm, he pulled her out of the lights and into the shadow of a large brick building. She leaned against the wall, and he placed both hands on either side of her head.

"Janelle," he said softly. "I wasn't accusing you of anything."

She lifted her eyes to his face. "No, you weren't accusing me, but you weren't sure whether to believe me, either."

He expelled a heavy breath, and a muscle jumped in his jaw. "I know it's not fair, Janelle, but I'm basically a mistrustful person. It goes with the job."

She regarded him thoughtfully. "Is it only the job, Alec, or is it me? Did Erin inflict so much damage that you can't trust any woman?"

Even in the dark, she saw anger transform his features. Then it disappeared as quickly as it had come, leaving his eyes empty and dull. "It's hard for me to trust," he said quietly. "When—when someone you care about lies to you . . . deliberately." He cleared his throat. "I caught her, Janelle. I caught her with another man . . . in our house. In our bed."

Janelle stared at him. It was the first time in her life that anyone had shared something so intimate, and so devastating, with her. It was the first time that a man had ever given her a part of himself. And she knew in that moment that what she felt for Alec Hayden was something she had never felt before. She wondered if this feeling was real love. "I would never lie to you, Alec. Never."

His eyes narrowed as he studied her hard, amazed that he really did believe her. She wasn't like anyone else he had ever known. She was unique.

He leaned close and pressed his upper body against her. As his mouth fastened over hers, he clasped her to him, and their hearts, full of *kefi* in this moment, began a rapid dance against each other.

"I want you, Janelle," he whispered harshly, his mouth forming the words against her lips. He lifted his hand to cover her breast. "Let's find a hotel . . ."

He was warm and strong and tasted of wine, and she felt her pulse thundering in her ears. His lips grazed a path down her throat. Oh, how she wanted to say yes. She wanted nothing more than to forget about the embassy and the monasteries and the murder that had consumed her and changed her life. She wanted only to lie in Alec's arms and explore the mystery of him. But the hands of some unseen ghost would not let go of his clutch on her. The fingers continued to squeeze her until she had no room left to breathe. Panic replaced the desire that had filled her only a second before.

She pushed Alec back and gazed, frightened, into his puzzled face. "I'm sorry," she whispered tearfully. "It's not you."

He nodded slowly. "You said you'd never lie to me, so I guess I have to believe you. Will you tell me what's wrong—what frightened you?"

She wrapped her arms around his waist and urged him closer. He came to her without a fight, and she laid her head against his chest. "I can't seem to get rid of the fear, Alec."

"Of me?"

She hugged him more tightly. "No, not of you. I constantly feel as if I'm being stalked, as if I'm going to be swallowed up by some unseen monster."

He pulled her head back and held it between his hands. His mouth dropped down to her lips and he kissed her gently and carefully. "I understand better than you might think," he said. "I feel the monsters, too. I want us to make them go away for each other. We can do that, you know…even if it's only for a little while. The way we did this afternoon."

She sighed. "If they went away, I'm not sure I could face them again. I want them to be gone forever. I don't want a temporary lull. Does that make sense?"

"I want to say no, but—yes, it does make sense."

"Did you mean what you said about our going away together—when this is all over?"

"Every word of it. I want you to lie beneath me and melt into my body. And . . . Janelle, I won't lie to you either." He lifted her chin with his fingers and smiled. "You've had a rare glimpse into this old impervious stone of a man. You've seen a part of me that I've never shown to anyone else." His smile faded into a frown as he stared at her. "Janelle? What's wrong? Are you okay?"

Her eyes were wide with disbelief. "What did you say?" she asked sharply.

"About what?"

"Rare glimpse . . ."

"What? Well, I—I said you've seen a part of—"

"Oh my God, Alec! No! I can't believe it!"

She pulled free, but he grasped her upper arms so she couldn't get away. "What are you talking about?"

"Rare glimpse, Alec. My God, he said those very words to me!"

"Who did?"

"Bluminfeld."

"What on earth are you talking about?"

"Alec, he showed me his collection the first day I arrived in Athens. It's been there in front of me all this time. I never thought—I never even made the connection. He—he told me that I was getting a rare glimpse—that few people ever got to see it." She was shaking her head back and forth, mumbling almost incoherently. "I don't believe it, I just don't believe—"

Alec gave her a small shake. "Got to see what, Janelle? What did Bluminfeld show you?"

"His collection, Alec!" She squeezed her eyes shut. "Of what?"

She kept shaking her head. It was Bluminfeld all along. The possibility had never entered her mind. Until now.

Janelle opened her eyes and gazed into Alec's intense stare. "Rare coins, Alec. James Bluminfeld has a priceless collection of rare, ancient coins."

Chapter Eleven

The town of Kalambaka nestled below a sheer cliff of the Pindos range. In the distance, the stark rock pillars rose ever higher from the plain, almost two thousand feet above sea level. Those stone needles, once believed to be meteors hurled by an angry god, filled Janelle with a strange sense of foreboding. Their twisted erosive shapes and the lofty solitude of the ancient monasteries had thwarted plunderers for a thousand years. They did not invite a close inspection.

Janelle sat back in her chair and sipped from the lemonade Josep Sklavopoulos's wife had prepared and brought out to her and Alec. They had left Thessaloniki immediately, Janelle catching a few hours' sleep in the car while Alec drove. He had stopped along the way to call Lefland and tell him about Bluminfeld. Thanks to Billy's uncanny ability to get answers and results, he had been able to give Alec the name and address of Mavro Sklavopoulos's brother in Kalambaka.

The tiny house and the lopsided terrace on which they now sat were cradled against the gray rocks of the mountains. A band of dark clouds billowed upward from behind them and slid in a slow threat across the sky.

"It was three days ago that he left?" Alec asked.

"Yes," Josep answered, twisting his glass between his hands. "My brother went up to Agios Petras on Tuesday."

Janelle watched the man carefully, trying to read truth or lies in the angles of his dark, lined face and in the timbre of his stilted English. She used to think it was so easy to know if someone was telling the truth, but no more. Involuntarily her eyes swung to Alec. She could only hope and pray that now she could tell the difference between honesty and deceit.

"And he hasn't returned?" she asked, looking back at Josep.

He slowly shook his head and sighed. "No. I am concerned. It is not like him."

Alec finished his lemonade and set the glass down on the small table. Josep's wife was immediately there to replenish it; then she once again faded back into the background of the house. "What did he say he was going to the monastery for?"

"Part of Agios Petras houses an orphanage. My brother Mavro is a benefactor—well, actually, there is this organization of men ... how you say ... "

"A fraternity?" Janelle offered.

"Yes, that is it. He belongs to this fraternity of men who are all benefactors of the orphanage."

"And the monks run this orphanage?" Alec asked.

"Yes. There are perhaps forty-five or fifty monks in Agios Petras, but only a few of them watch over the thirty orphans."

"Who's in charge of the monastery?" Janelle asked.

"Father Gregouriou. He has been there for over forty years. He may or may not take visitors." Josep shrugged and added vaguely, "It all depends."

Alec picked up the fresh glass of lemonade. "Did Mavro say—" He paused as a growl of thunder rumbled in the distant sky. "Did he say if any of the other benefactors were going to meet him there?"

"This I do not know, but..." Josep frowned at the untouched glass between his hands. "It is strange, yes?"

"What is?"

"My brother—Mavro—the way he behaved. He was—well, he was acting very strangely."

Alec and Janelle exchanged a quick glance. "In what way?" she asked.

"He spoke of his job in Athens—with the Department of Antiquities. He spoke of quitting."

"Had he ever talked of this before?"

Josep shook his head and looked from Alec to Janelle and back again. "No. Never. I thought my brother was very happy in his job. But now it appears not so."

Alec leaned forward in his chair and rested his forearms on his knees. "He gave you no hints—no clues to anything that might be wrong at the ministry?"

"No. He said only that he had made enough money to retire and that he believed he would do this. I find that particularly strange. My brother did not make very much money with the government. He could come back to Kalambaka and farm, but..." Josep smiled wistfully. "My brother is not a farmer. I do not know how he could live here. So, yes, it is strange. And I am worried."

The silence that hung over the terrace was punctuated by distant claps of thunder. The sky was the color of lead. A few clouds now covered the tops of the rock formations.

Alec finally spoke. "We want to see your brother, Josep. We want to go up to the monastery and see if we can find him."

"You believe that my brother is in trouble, yes?"

Alec saw the flitting shadow of the wife dart away from the open door. He looked back at Josep. "I hope not, Mr. Sklavopoulos. But I am afraid he might be."

Janelle couldn't miss the look of pain that distorted the man's dark features. She wished that she and Alec had not been the ones to put it there. "This road," she said, "the one that leads through the village—will it take us up to the monastery?"

Josep turned toward her and composed his tired features into a polite smile. "Yes. It is about four kilometers to the top. A circular road will take you through the forest. But Agios Petras is connected to the main cliff by a footbridge, so you will have to stop your car and walk the remainder of the way."

Alec polished off the second glass of lemonade in one swallow. "There are other monasteries up in the mountains, aren't there?"

"Oh, yes, but none in—how you say?—operation." Josep waited for Alec's nod before continuing. "There is Agios Nikolaos, Agia Roussani, Triada, Varlaam, and of course the Great Meteoran itself."

"But aren't they only ruins?" Janelle asked.

"Yes, I am afraid so. A nunnery exists in Agios Stephanos, with perhaps twenty nuns. Until only a few years ago, women were not allowed on the Holy

Mountain. It is still so on Mount Athos. But here—
well, time is more modern, yes?''

"You mean if I wanted to go to the monasteries on
Mount Athos—even for a visit—I would not be allowed?''

"No. Cruise ships are forbidden to approach within
five hundred meters if women are on board.''

Janelle noticed Alec's empty glass on the table and
then saw that his foot was wiggling. She ignored his
impatience. "How did the monasteries get to be built
on those tall rocks? It's such a forbidding place.''

"I do not know. I am only a farmer. But they have
been there for a long time, to guard against soldiers.
The mountains are very hard to climb. And now—''
Josep glanced at Alec, who was standing and jingling
the change in his pockets. "I see that you must go.''

Janelle stood, also, but refused to let Alec's impatience make her be impolite. "Yes, but please tell your
wife thank you for the drink. You are most hospita-
ble.''

Josep beamed proudly. "And you are most welcome anytime in my humble home.''

THE ROAD WOUND UPWARD through the dense, pine-
clad forest, leaving the graceful olive groves below.
Gigantic pillars of stone, split and twisted by the erosive power of the sea, rose two thousand feet above in
an unearthly row.

Janelle glanced over at Alec. His hands were
gripped tightly on the wheel as he concentrated on
each curve of the road. "Mavro must have made
plenty of money in this smuggling operation if he's
considering retirement. But doesn't it seem as if Boris

would want him to stay with the department? How could he help with the smuggling otherwise?''

Alec shrugged and kept his eyes on the road. ''Maybe he realized he was expendable.''

''Do you think he's dead, then?''

Alec shrugged. ''I don't know. If he tried to get out the way Nikos did, he probably is. It appears that once you're involved in this business, you're in it for life.''

The clouds above the mountains grew darker. As the road curved and the line of trees broke, the view stretched over the vast plain all the way to the sea. To the north and west rose the snow-covered peaks of Olympus and Pindos, while below lay orchards of almond and peach trees, just beginning to bloom. Sprouts of green corn dotted the soil; other fields, farther away and toward the sea, were covered with flaming red poppies. The road swerved sharply again, and there, perched high on a pinnacle, was Agios Petras, thrusting its massive walls above the cliff.

Alec stopped the car, and he and Janelle both sat silently for a minute, gazing in awe at the ancient suspended bridge they had to cross on foot to reach the monastery. It creaked and groaned from its worn hinges as it swung over a sheer abyss. Janelle felt a quiver of apprehension when they climbed out and peered down the steep canyon walls. ''How strong is your faith?'' she asked.

Alec tested the first rickety board with his foot. ''Growing blinder by the minute.'' He took another step, then another. ''Stay right behind me and step where I do.''

Behind him, Janelle watched where he placed his feet and made sure hers landed on the same spots. She tried to think of nothing else, tried not to look down

at the gaping abyss below or to imagine the sensation
of falling onto the sharp rocks. She concentrated only
on following Alec's footsteps.

She looked up once at the group of buildings ahead.
Each one rose from a different level. Some were
whitewashed; others were built from stone and brick.
Agios Petras was dark stone. Connecting each struc-
ture were wooden galleries and balconies that hung
precariously over the yawning chasm.

A thundercloud cracked above, causing Janelle to
lose her balance and lurch forward. Alec swung
around and steadied her, and she could see the vapor
of his breath, quick and agitated in the cold, cloud-
covered air. She regained her balance, pulled her green
cardigan sweater more tightly around her, and continued forward, carefully watching Alec's steps.

Finally they reached the other side. Neither of them
could speak. They looked back at the bridge they had
crossed and then stared at each other, in awe of the
feat they had just accomplished. Wordlessly, Alec
took her hand and they began to climb the steep stairway that was cut into the rock of the cliff. Above them
was the entrance to the monastery.

At the top of the stairs, they followed a flat stone
path through an archway into a courtyard filled with
flowers. The fountain in the middle of the courtyard
had long since ceased to run, and the stone figure in its
center was missing an arm. A cord hung from a bell at
the carved wooden door. Alec pulled on it.

When no one appeared, he tugged on the cord
again. "I wonder if anybody is home."

"I think the wheels turn very slowly in a place like
this," Janelle murmured.

Moments later the door was opened. In the dim rectangle of light stood an old man in a black robe and a black cylindrical hat. *"Ne?"*

"Kalimera," Alec said, smiling. "Do you speak English?"

The old man nodded. "I do."

Janelle sighed with relief. Although languages came easily to her, she had decided that Greek was going to be a real challenge.

"My name is Alec Hayden. I am with the United States government."

The man's expression remained fixed, but he pushed his thick round glasses up higher on the bridge of his nose. "And I am Father Gregouriou. But we do not deal in governments here at Agios Petras."

"Yes," Alec said. "I know. But we are looking for a man who supposedly has come here—about the orphanage. Mavro Sklavopoulos. Do you know him?"

"Yes, I know him."

"May we talk to you about him?"

Father Gregouriou stepped aside and motioned for them to enter. Once they were inside, their eyes gradually adjusted to the dimness. The stone floor was laced with light from the arched windows, but as the clouds rolled in and grew blacker, the lacework shifted and retreated into darkness. They followed the silent aged figure as he went down winding corridors, past other men in black robes and cylindrical hats. The corridor fanned out into a wide room with hallways leading off at every angle. A pair of double doors opened into a small church, and the sounds of voices raised in prayer met their ears. Chandeliers gleamed, and the bronze eagle of Byzantium hovered over a tiny alcove. Monks bowed, prostrated themselves and lit candles while they sang in an antiphonal chant.

Father Gregouriou did not stop. He continued to lead Janelle and Alec down another long corridor in which tapestries of martyrs and saints looked down upon them from the walls. Eventually they reached a doorway to a flower-lined balcony overlooking the courtyard.

"You will have brandy?" Father Gregouriou asked.

"Yes," Alec answered. "Thank you."

There was no signal that they could discern, no ringing of a bell, no calling of a servant. But the moment they sat down in woven chairs on the balcony, a black-robed monk appeared with three glasses of brandy and a plate of bread.

"Mavro Sklavopoulos was here for only a day," Father Gregouriou said, as if there had been no lull in the conversation, as if the quarter hour of traversing winding hallways and listening to the chants of monks and being served bread and brandy had never taken place.

"He came about the orphanage?" Janelle asked, but the monk kept his face and his answer directed solely at Alec. Women were not welcome, she remembered. Only tolerated.

"He comes once a month. He and the others. They give much money to our orphanage. Without them, it would not exist."

Alec lifted his glass and took a sip of brandy. "You said others. Do you have their names?"

"No. They wish to remain anonymous. Mavro Sklavopoulos is their intermediary. He is seemingly the one in charge."

Janelle glanced at Alec, but he was watching the monk. "So they brought you money for the orphanage," he said. "When was this?"

"Three days ago."

"And then where did they go?"

Father Gregouriou's eyes scanned the darkening horizon. "These mountains are full of places for retreat. What those men do outside my monastery is not of importance to me. I am concerned only with what takes place within these walls."

A strong wind began to blow and howl. The balconies creaked on their ancient hinges. The sky grew completely dark, and the air that whipped across their faces was moist with tiny droplets of water.

"Are you saying that you have no idea where they went, Father?" Janelle persisted, even though she knew his answer would be directed to Alec.

His yellowed eyes never budged. He pushed the glasses higher on his nose with gnarled fingers. "The Great Meteoran is a favorite spot for meditation. Perhaps you should look there."

A bell clanged in the courtyard, and soon the monks filed out, one by one. Alec set down his glass of brandy and stood up, reaching for Janelle's hand. Father Gregouriou stood, also. Another bell tinkled somewhere else.

"A signal for prayer in the dining room," the old monk explained. "And then a brother will read a lesson against gluttony."

They walked through the doors and down a different corridor from the one before. "This is our library," Father Gregouriou said when Janelle paused in a wide doorway. "We have many classical and medieval manuscripts."

"And the relics in the glass cases?" she asked.

He looked directly at Alec. "A piece of cloth that Mary dropped at Calvary. A part of the crown of thorns. Sacred treasures."

They followed him down the hallway until he stopped before a closed door. "This is my hut, where I live and carve my wooden icons."

"How long have you lived here, Father?" Alec asked.

"Fifty years." He walked on. "I used to live with two other monks in the hut."

"Where are they now?"

"They sleep. I miss them sometimes."

JANELLE SAT IN THE COURTYARD and waited for Alec to finish his tour. Father Gregouriou had offered to show him more of the monastery, places that were still off-limits to a woman. Alec could not refuse. Janelle could not go.

The flowers around the courtyard were well tended, and she wondered if it was only a lack of funds that kept the empty fountain from operating. The wind grew colder as she sat there; and the air was heavy with moisture. Something rustled in the bushes behind her, and she turned quickly, looking back over her shoulder. It was only the wind shaking the leaves.

Soon she noticed a pair of eyes watching her from behind a column on the far side of the courtyard. The eyes continued to stare at her until she smiled, and then a young boy's small feet sent him scurrying back into the darkened corridors of the monastery.

Janelle smiled to herself and thought about what it would be like to grow up in this high, remote spot. Were the children in the orphanage being prepared only for life in a monastery or a nunnery? Since they were so isolated, how could it be otherwise?

She looked up at the weathered facades of the monastery buildings. Pinpoints of lamplight in the cells silhouetted monks in prayers of repentance. The windows rattled with each breath of the cold wind.

Again something stirred in the bushes behind her, and she spun around to see who it was. There was no one. And yet she felt sure that she was being watched, no doubt by another young orphan who must find her—a female dressed in a kelly-green cardigan sweater and a beige skirt—a wonderfully dangerous curiosity in this world of black-robed men.

She heard the rustle behind her again, but this time she was given no chance to turn around. A man with graying hair and the features of a hawk sat down beside her on the chipped stone bench. She looked at him, startled, but it was only after he began to speak that she felt fear, more intense and immediate than what she had experienced so far, creep along the surface of her skin.

"Janelle Lindsey, I warned you, did I not?" He paused as if he was waiting for her answer, but she had none to give him. This man, Boris, had the power in his voice alone to destroy her ability to speak and think. "I told you that I wanted the coin. But you did not listen. You hid from me. Now we have found each other."

Janelle's eyes automatically searched the far corner of the courtyard for Alec. He was nowhere to be seen.

Boris stood and grasped her upper arm, pulling her with surprising gentleness to her feet. She looked at his face. The gentleness masked an evil that sent an icy shudder through her body. His hand felt cold even through her sweater and blouse.

A clap of thunder issued from the clouds above them, the air became almost too thick with moisture for Janelle to catch her breath. As a few fat raindrops started to fall, she glanced at the fountain and wondered, irrationally, if the rain would fill it.

There was the sound of a metallic click, and her gaze dropped down to Boris's right hand. The barrel of his gun was only a fraction of an inch from her waist.

He smiled. "You will come with me now, Janelle Lindsey?"

She felt the slight tug on her arm as he guided her out the courtyard toward the stone pathway that led through the bushes and away from the monastery. She heard another loud rustling noise in the bushes and swung her head toward the sound. She saw nothing, but she knew now that someone was indeed watching them. It had not been Boris in the shrubs; it was most probably not a young orphan, either.

Janelle felt the tip of the gun against her waist, and the pressure of Boris's hand on her arm increased.

The rain began to fall. With any thoughts of escape or struggle now frozen at the spot where the gun barrel touched her, Janelle could do nothing but let the Russian lead her away from the monastery, away from Alec and away from any good chance of survival.

Chapter Twelve

It was as if Janelle were in a closed windowless room. She could hear the rain pounding outside, beating against the walls, but nothing penetrated the locked room. She felt nothing, even though Boris was dragging her over the rain-soaked rocks, leading her up higher and higher toward some unknown destination. She had to fight this deadly stupor, fight her way out of the fog of despondency enveloping her. She didn't want to die. She didn't want to be dragged away like a lamb to slaughter. She had been dragged and pulled and coerced all her life. She had always been a lamb, it seemed. She did not want to die the same way.

Boris slipped on a wet rock and Janelle jerked her arm, pulling free of him. But within less than two seconds, he had her in his grasp again. And he was laughing. "Come now, Miss Lindsey. No heroics, please."

She tried hard not to let the despondency win out. "Where are you taking me?" she managed to shout through the rain as she attempted once again to struggle free of his grasp.

"Not much farther. Here. This way." He kept his fingers clutched tightly around her upper arm, squeezing the flesh through her sweater. The gun never left her side. "Here we are." He led her toward a building that looked empty and had been left to ruin. Janelle assumed it was one of the several other monasteries that had been abandoned years before.

Boris pushed her in through the door. The rain beat hard against the rotting wood, and the wind buffeted the creaking outer walls. Two men were waiting inside. Janelle came to a stop in the center of a large, dismal room. The two men stood in front of her, Boris behind her. As she shifted her weight, she felt a loose floorboard move beneath her feet. She stared at the strangers. A week ago, she might have said they were Greek. But now she realized how difficult it was to discern the subtle differences in some people. Like Zafer, one of the men was dark, with heavy brows and a mustache. Perhaps he was Turkish. Perhaps, like Boris Ivanov, he was Russian. The other man was lighter skinned and had very little hair. But when he spoke, she knew positively that he, too, was Russian.

"Does she have it?" he asked in Russian. Janelle stared at him but gave no sign that she had understood. Maybe it would be better that way. Maybe by pretending that she didn't understand what they were saying, she could hold them off for a little longer. It might be her only chance.

Boris stepped out from behind her and joined his accomplices. He smiled and spoke in English. "You will give it to us now, Miss Lindsey."

As she stood there in the middle of the crumbling room, with the rain pounding against the building and the wind howling like a lone wolf over the rocks, Janelle felt a raw chill close around her and not only because her clothes were soaking wet. What would happen when Alec came back to the courtyard and discovered she was gone? Where would he look? What would he do to find her? He might be too late after all. *Janelle Lindsey, staff assistant to the American chargé d'affaires to Greece, suspected murderer and fugitive from the police, has disappeared in the mountains of Thessaly without a trace.*

"I don't have it," she finally said, looking straight into Boris's eyes.

"Then we must see for ourselves, of course. You do understand, do you not?"

Janelle's body stiffened as the two men stepped forward quickly and grabbed her arms. "Why is it so important?" she asked, trying desperately to think of a way out. "Is it for Bluminfeld? For his collection? Is it payment for his part in this?"

Boris laughed lightly. "You are stalling, Miss Lindsey. It will do you no good, of course. Still," he mused, pacing back and forth as he studied her, "I am surprised. We didn't expect you to be so . . . so perceptive. We were under the impression that you would be an easy victim."

"We? You mean you and James Bluminfeld?"

"It was supposed to be a simple thing to set you up as the murderer of Nikos Marinatos."

"But you didn't realize I would have the coin."

"No, that we did not realize." Boris studied her again, this time with respect. "We underestimated you, Miss Lindsey."

Another voice cut across the room from the doorway. "And I underestimated you, Ivanov. Is this the way you treat women in Moscow?"

Janelle, surprised to hear that particular voice, swung around and stared at Alec. He was standing just inside the door. The rain dripped from his hair and clothes, forming a pool on the floor at his feet.

He stepped in farther and smiled. "Beats me how your country's population is growing."

Janelle looked back at Boris. He, too, was smiling. "Ah, it is you," he said, sounding pleased.

Alec walked across the room to Boris. "Lesson one with women, Ivanov. If you want something, you have to be charming." He pulled the coin from his pocket and grinned. "Voilà!" He tossed it, and Boris caught it in his left hand. The gun was still clutched in his right hand.

Boris examined the coin closely, then stuck it into his own pocket. He looked at Alec. "So...something for nothing. Quite a bargain coming from you, Alec Hayden. You, of course, deserve something for your trouble with the girl."

Janelle's mouth had fallen open, and her heart was beating too fast. His trouble with the girl? If you want something, you have to be charming? Alec. He had been with them all the time. He was part of the operation. God, how could she have been so stupid!

Alec was about to say something to Boris when Janelle's shriek cut through the air. She had yanked her arms free of the two men and was pounding her fists against Alec's chest and into his face. "You thief!" she yelled. "You traitor! You bastard!"

Alec tried to dodge the blows and reach for her at the same time, but the two Russians got to her first. They yanked her backward and pulled her arms behind her back, holding tightly to her squirming body.

"Get her out of here," Boris shouted in Russian.

"Where do we take her?" they asked.

"To the cells."

The men stalled. "In this weather?"

"Take her, dammit. Now. And wait up there with her. Guard her until I am finished here, and then we will decide what to do with her."

Alec looked as if he was about to reach for her again, but she kicked at him and he stepped back, as if surprised by her reaction. She was directly in front of him, yet she couldn't read his expression. It wasn't one of contriteness or fear or—anything. It was blank. She glared at him. "God, what a fool I was to think you were special! You're worse than Nikos ever was!"

Before he could answer, the men spirited Janelle out the door and into the rain.

Inside the room, Alec turned toward Boris. His expression was as blank as before, his eyes as frigid gray as the sky, but his voice sliced through the air like the cold blade of a knife. "If you or your men hurt her in any way, I will kill you, Ivanov."

Boris's eyes held a wary glint as he stared at Alec.

Alec's jaw was hard. "I will cut you into a thousand pieces and leave you on the rocks for the buzzards."

There was only a moment of hesitation before Boris regained his composure. He chuckled. "How will you do that, Alec Hayden, when you too will be dead? Now, please hand me your weapon."

Alec glanced toward the doorway through which Janelle had gone, still hearing the echo of her bitter words. "How long has this been going on—this smuggling?"

"A long time. The weapon—now."

Alec stooped over and lifted one pant leg. Secured in the holster strapped to his calf was a Colt 380 Government automatic. He unfastened the holster and pulled the gun free, tossing it onto the floor at Ivanov's feet. "Byzantine relics. Why?"

Boris retrieved the gun and stuck it in his coat pocket. "They belong to the Russian people."

"How do you figure that?"

Ivanov waved his own gun loosely. "When Constantinople fell, Moscow took over as the center of Christendom." He shrugged. "By virtue of that dominance, the relics are ours."

Alec snorted. "Christian relics? Aren't you scrambling ideologies a bit?"

"The only ideology that counts, Alec Hayden, is the one that gives you money and power. Anything else is pure fantasy."

"I see." Alec watched Boris switch the gun from one hand to the other. It was obvious the Russian was nervous, and at this point Alec wasn't sure if that was good or bad. Nervous men were unpredictable. "And Bluminfeld?" he asked, stalling for time. "How long has he been involved with you?"

Boris leaned back against the wall, seemingly amused by the questions. "Again, for a long time," he answered. "I met James in sixty-seven when he was on special assignment to Budapest. An acquaintance of mine had dealt in the antiquities market with him many times in the past. Your Mr. Bluminfeld has had a propensity for this sort of thing. Did you know he was an art-history major? No? Yes, he was. And he also received his master's in the art of the Byzantine Empire in Istanbul. I knew from his past dealings that he was, shall we say, easily corruptible. When he took over the embassy in your ambassador's absence, things could not have been better."

Ivanov's smile was smug, but Alec noticed that he now had a firmer grip on the gun, as if he had a definite goal in mind. "And Nikos?"

Boris shrugged. "A minor player, I assure you. Not at all necessary to the overall picture."

"He wanted out, so you killed him."

Boris laughed. "I? Hardly."

"Then who?"

The Russian lifted his chin and laughed. "You wish to know much before you die, don't you?" He waved the gun at him. "That is an interesting thing about you, Alec Hayden. Of course, I have dealt with you only once or twice, but I know of you very well. You are very inquisitive, almost compulsively so. An impatient man, too, unwilling to bend, unwilling to tolerate anything less than perfection in people you work with, in friends you deal with...in your women." Boris regarded him closely. "Miss Lindsey does not seem your type. She is much too—too delicate for such an impatient man as you. But then, that is the way with so many of you Americans. A very impatient people."

"I can be patient, Ivanov. I can wait as long as it takes for you to tell me everything."

Boris chuckled. "Oh, you do amuse me, Alec Hayden. You are very patient when it comes to your own demise." He chuckled again. "And I suppose that you would also like to see what we have stored here in the monastery—before you...depart."

Alec's mouth formed a half smile. "Indulge me, Boris."

"Of course," he answered with that same overconfident superiority. "Why not?" He waved the gun again. "It is quite a walk from here. And in this storm..."

Alec's smile grew broader. "I don't mind the rain."

Boris laughed heartily. "Of course you don't. Well then, let us go, you and I." He raised the gun and pointed it directly at Alec. "Shall we?"

Alec pivoted on his heels and, with Ivanov's gun at his back, walked out into the raging storm.

Chapter Thirteen

Janelle drew her legs up for warmth and huddled back against the rocks in a vain attempt to keep warm. The dampness seeped through every pore in her body and wrapped its icy claws around her bones. The wind was ferocious at this altitude; it whipped against her, driving her farther back against the cold, wet rocks.

She was in one of the ancient monastic prison cells where Boris had instructed the men to take her. In actuality, the cells were not as she had expected them to be. They were nothing like the one in Athens in which she had spent that long, lonely night. These were mere shallow caves, situated by nature at a dizzying height. Those transgressors of long ago had been forced, as she was now, to crouch on the narrow ledge, exposed to the harsh elements for perhaps endless periods of time. She wondered how long she could possibly last.

Far below her lay the almond and peach fields that she and Alec had driven past earlier today. But now they lay blanketed under the heavy gray clouds. To the left and several hundred feet below was Agios Petras, where Alec had left her to be captured by his partner, Boris Ivanov. No, she wasn't going to think about that. It didn't matter. She forced the painful thought away and looked up. About a hundred yards to her right, hollowed out of the rock and perched like an unreachable eagle's nest, was the Great Meteoran, once the largest and most magnificent monastery on the Holy Mountain and now only a shell of its former glorious self.

Janelle lowered her head and tucked it into the wet folds of her skirt. Her two captors sat nearby, grumbling in Russian over whatever fates had forced them to endure this kind of abuse. "Boris," one of them spat. "That wretched cur. Who does he think we are that he can do this to us?"

"Shut up," the other one warned. "You know he has ears everywhere. If he hears you, we, too, will die."

Janelle remained still, never letting on that she understood a word they were saying. It wasn't that she had a plan for escape in mind. Instead, it was simply that she was beyond caring. The cold and the rain and the wind had made her numb. She didn't want to have to think about anything. She didn't want to die. But even more than that, she didn't want to think.

"Were do you suppose he is now?" one of the men asked.

"Who?"

"Boris."

"Who knows," the second man answered, his tone filled with disdain. "Probably up there with his treasures."

Janelle lifted her head, hoping to see which way the man was looking. His gaze was directed straight over the edge of the cliff into the low-lying clouds. She dropped her head back to her knees, and the unwanted thoughts returned. Alec had betrayed her. She had believed, stupidly enough, that he cared for her. He was so gentle, so warm. He had told her he would never lie, never lie, never lie . . .

The two Russians continued their grumbling and complaints about the odious task they were assigned to perform. "What do you suppose he will want done with her?"

Janelle's shoulders grew tense, and she could almost hear the other man shrug as if the outcome were of no consequence whatsoever. "Tossed over the cliff, I imagine."

The first speaker was silent for a moment, then said, "It's a shame, you know. Not to take advantage of this."

The other man hesitated while he glanced over at Janelle. "Forget it. We have more important things to think about. Tonight we must package up the rest of the cargo. Tomorrow, it leaves for Athos."

Janelle slowly raised her head and listened. She had not wanted to think about what was going to happen to her, or what would happen to the stolen relics. She had convinced herself that it no longer mattered. And yet it did. She had spent every conscious moment thinking about her situation and the gold coin for the past week. She could not now shut those thoughts off as if they were nothing more substantial than a flow of water from a tap.

The men would not like it if they knew that she could understand them. But she did understand. The cargo would leave tomorrow for Athos. It was here now, somewhere up there. She stared up through the rain at the Great Meteoran. Somewhere in that monastic ruin were the treasures. She lowered her eyes and

gazed out at nothing, but listened carefully to everything the men were saying.

And they said a great deal. Janelle's only problem
was how to get away from them. If she could escape,
then maybe, just maybe, she could do something to
stop Boris and Alec. She might die trying, but it would
be no different if she stayed with these two men. They
were going to kill her in the end anyway. Remaining
numb would solve nothing.

To the right and above her was a narrow plateau
covered by a patch of scrubby pines. If she could get
up there...

She stared at the two men huddled back against the
rocks beside her. The rain had increased, and now it
was hard to hear what they were saying. "I need to go
up there," she said.

They looked over at her blankly.

She pointed to the plateau above the ledge and
shouted over the noise of the driving rain. "Up there.
Toilet."

The Russians looked at each other, frowning as they
mumbled something she couldn't hear.

They continued to talk between themselves, and she
began to wonder if they had forgotten what she had
said. She could make them understand, but if they realized she spoke Russian, it was likely they wouldn't
wait for Ivanov's instructions to kill her. They
wouldn't want to risk the possibility that she had heard
them talking about Boris or the cargo of stolen relics.
They would do away with her immediately.

The men turned back to her, and the balding one
stood up. He motioned Janelle to stand, also. She
forced her chilled bones into an upright position and
felt her arm grasped in his huge claw. Together they

moved carefully along the precipitous ledge, side by side, his hand around her arm, as they clung to the rocks for support. All it would take was one false step, one fumbling handhold on the rocks, and the wind would brush them off the cliff as if they were a loose piece of stone.

After they had reached the narrow rock stairway that led up to the plateau, the Russian thrust Janelle up in front of him, pushing her and clinging to her at the same time. They made it to the plateau and hunkered down into the bushes, trying to dodge the heavy rain that cascaded down in driving sheets.

Janelle pointed to the far side of the plateau. "May I go over there?"

At first she thought he didn't understand, but finally he released her arm and pointed in the same direction. Then, nodding, he squatted lower in a vain attempt to escape the cold. But she knew, as she walked away from him, that he was watching every move she made.

She reached the far side and stopped, turning around to stare at him. They remained this way for a moment or two, both refusing to back down. Then he shrugged and turned his back to her, keeping low against the scrubby pine.

Time was precious now. Janelle didn't have a second to waste. If she was going to get away, she would have to do it now. She swung around, trying to get her bearings. She had to climb up to the monastery. She had no idea what she would do once she got there and found the treasures. All she knew was that she had to stop Boris. Had to stop Alec. It would be her only chance to vindicate herself, her only chance to prove that she was an innocent pawn in this deadly game. Provided she could stay alive.

Through the wet slate curtain that hung all around her, she thought she could make out a pathway leading up the face of the tallest rock needle. Maybe it was only a distortion caused by the wind and rain, maybe her fear made her see it the way she did, but whatever caused the image to appear, the rock stairway looked as if it were almost perpendicular to the ground. How could she do it? How could she ever climb up the face of that needle without being whipped by the wind into the chasm below?

She looked back at her captor. He was still facing the opposite direction, still waiting for her. Could she make it to the stairway without his seeing her? Could she flee from two men who were twice her size and weight and who had no qualms about killing her? Could she actually do it? At least they were not carrying guns, as Boris had been. But the harnesses they wore wrapped around their waists and thighs held knives. Very large knives by the looks of them. Still, that was to her benefit. Even if the man was an excellent thrower, he could never hit her in this rain. A bullet would have been a different matter.

Without another thought to drain away more precious seconds, Janelle took off through the wind-swirled rain, running as fast as she could away from her captors, away from the men whose job it was to end her life.

She heard a shout behind her, muffled and distorted by the wind, but still a sound that told her she had not escaped unnoticed. She looked over her shoulder and saw him coming after her. She had not fooled him for a minute. But she wasn't about to stop now. Her fate would be sealed for certain if he caught up with her.

She was quite a distance ahead of him, at least fifty yards, and if she could just reach the steep stairway and make it up to the top, maybe she could lose him.

Janelle ran on. She wasted no more time by turning around to see where he was. He was behind her. That was all she needed to know. The path was a thin line between the scrub pine, and it was relatively straight. The rain slapped against her face, stinging her flesh. Her breath made short clouds of vapor in front of her. All sounds of the mountains were lost in the torrential downpour. Only the wind could be heard as it whipped her hair and clothes.

She kept on going until she came to the rock stairway. It was as steep up close as it had appeared from across the plateau. It had not been an optical illusion after all. Beside the rock cliff was a heavy rope, worn every couple of inches to a few thin strands. She had heard stories of how monks once used ropes and nets to pull young novices up to the reclusive nests of the monasteries. This rope had probably been used specifically for that purpose. It was that old. It probably would not support her weight.

She swallowed her fear and blindly grabbed hold of it. She lifted one foot to the first high step and used the rope to help her pull her other foot up. The wind battered against her. Janelle took another step, knowing that a fear of death at the hands of her captors was the only thing that gave her the courage to keep moving. One excruciating step followed another. She had made it almost halfway up when she looked back and saw both men coming along the path. The dark one, the one who had remained behind at the prison cells, was lagging far behind the other.

The fierce wind lashed at Janelle; the driving rain bit at her exposed flesh. Her stockings were shredded and the strap on one of her sandals had broken. Her wet clothes hung on her body, weighting her down. It took all the strength she had to grasp the rope and pull herself up another step.

By some miracle other than her own strength, Janelle made it to the top. Swinging her right leg up over the ledge, she clutched onto the boulders at the top, pulling her other leg up and over. Then she looked down and saw that the balding man was approaching the rock stairway. She could run, but he would still climb up and resume his chase.

All energy left her in a painful rush. She couldn't go on. She was too tired to run anymore. If he caught up with her and killed her, so be it. Dammit, she was just too tired to keep going.

What it was that poked and prodded at her lethargy, urging her to get up and keep going despite the odds, she didn't know. But something—some deep-seated desire to live—shoved the fatigue aside and spun her into action.

She looked down again and saw the man almost at the base of the cliff. There was only one thing to do. It would use up valuable time and might prove to be impossible, but it was the only thing she could think of, the only way to stop them from climbing up after her.

Slowly and laboriously, she began to tug on the heavy rope, hoping he hadn't reached it yet. She grasped it first with her right hand and pulled, then crossed over with her left and tugged again, hauling it inch by infinitesimal inch up the rock face. Groaning and straining, she pulled at the rope until she thought her lungs would burst from the effort. When the end of the rope came up in her hands, she stared at it in disbelief. She had done the impossible. She had actually had the strength to do it.

The balding man had reached the bottom of the rock needle and was gazing up in astonishment. But his surprise immediately gave way to anger, and his enraged cry carried up in the eddies of the wind to her ears. The other man was still running fast, and within seconds he, too, would be at the foot of the stairway.

Janelle stood up and started to run again. She could just make out the ghostly outline of the stone monastery in the distance, beyond a small plateau. Then it appeared that she would have to cross a rock ledge to get to it. But she couldn't stop. Even though the scent of death clogged her nose and throat, she could not stop. Not now. Not after coming this far.

At that moment from behind her, a strangled cry, shrill and terrible, vibrated on the wind. It was a wail that was so solitary and so piercing that Janelle stopped dead in her tracks, unable to move. A shudder rippled through her body, wrenching the breath from her lungs and shaking her to the very soul. The shattered sound had ceased, but in its wake was the haunting reverberation of the wind's own cry.

Her arms crossed protectively in front of her. One of her captors had not made it up the cliff. The rope had anchored her to the rocks, held her safe from the wind's ferocious whip. Not so for the man behind her.

Instinct and the need to survive pushed her onward. At the far edge of the plateau, she looked back and saw the second man coming. Somehow he had made it up the stairway without the rope. Janelle's pause lasted only a few seconds before she started across the ledge. Its length was shorter than she had at first imagined, and when she made it around the bend, she found herself on another pathway, this one cut deep into the rocks and leading up at a forty-five-degree angle.

She heard a shout from the man behind her. He yelled for her to stop, and she could tell that he was not that far behind her now. Her lungs felt as if they were going to explode, and she had a painful stitch in her side. Her hands, where they grasped the slippery rocks for support, were numb from the cold. Only a steady ache throbbed through the joints of her fingers. She felt cold tears slide down her face, but the even colder rain washed them away. Her hair streamed into her face, and she constantly had to brush it away in order to see where she was going.

She was reaching for the next rock to help her along the steep pathway when she heard something whistle through the air beside her and stop with a vibrating twang. She looked down and stared at the steel blade of the knife that was stuck in the crevasse between two rocks. It had missed her by less than a foot.

Stunned, she spun around. The dark man was running up the path behind her, grabbing onto the same rocks she had grasped to help him make the climb. He was only a few feet away when he stopped, panting breathlessly. They stared at each other. Neither of them moved. Neither dared. Only the short bursts of vapor from their lungs traveled between them. Janelle could taste his fear as well as her own. The man was glaring at her, and she knew that he wanted nothing more than to kill her, to make her pay for what she had done to his friend.

His stare dropped to the knife still stuck between the two rocks. Janelle's eyes followed. Her moment of hesitation was almost too long. Yet some unseen force propelled her into action. She grabbed for the knife, but it was wedged tightly in the crevasse. It would not come free. The man was moving toward her, his words incoherent in the low growl that came from his throat. She yanked hard, and this time the knife loosened. She pulled her hand back and the knife came with it.

The man was in front of her now and he reached out. Janelle instinctively swung her arm upward to avoid his grasp. There was a momentary look of surprise on his face, and then Janelle saw the blood on his arm. She cried out in fear and took a step backward, but he came at her again, the growl alternating between an ominous hiss.

She jumped back again and almost lost her balance. He took advantage of the moment and grabbed for the knife. She swung her arm in the same arc as before, but this time her foot slipped on the wet rocks. She stumbled forward and fell into the man's arms. The knife hit something—something that yielded, that felt odd against the pressure of her hand and made a strange sound unlike any she had ever heard before.

The man opened his mouth to speak, but nothing came out. Realizing now that she was in his arms, Janelle screamed and jumped back, pulling the knife with her. This time, it made a wet sucking sound.

Her mouth dropped open in shock as she stared incredulously at the blood-soaked blade in her hand. Numbed by something beyond the cold wind and rain, Janelle lifted her eyes to the man's face. His mouth was still moving wordlessly, and he gaped at her as if he couldn't believe what she had done. He sat back on a large boulder, looking as if he had just sat down for a short rest. His hand came up and covered the spot on his chest. He lifted the hand slowly up and stared at the red fingers. Then he looked up at Janelle once more and very slowly sank to the ground, his eyes still staring at her and his mouth still moving around the silent words that would not come.

Hypnotized by the steady beat of the rain, the relentless howl of the wind and the sight of the man in front of her, Janelle stood perfectly still in the middle of the pathway. A remote curiosity filtered into her brain, a mind-boggling inquisitiveness that refused to let in any acknowledgment of her part in this. She studied the man as if he were a biological phenomenon. People didn't die this way. Death was meant to startle, to wrestle life from one's body, to wrench the breath from the lungs and instantly still the beat of the heart. Death was not a slow, quiet settling to the earth. Death did not leave one surprised, dazed, trying to speak.

Janelle's hand jerked open spasmodically and froze. The knife fell to the ground at her feet. She watched in fascination as the man's gaze lowered to the blade, but he made no move to retrieve it. His eyelids did not lift again.

Janelle opened her mouth and screamed again and again, but no sound came from her constricted throat. Frantically she turned and clawed at the boulders as she tried to make her way along the steep path, leaping from rock to slippery rock, tearing her clothes and flesh on the sharp pine branches. The fear that now consumed her was coiled so tightly within her chest that she expected it to spring loose at any minute and fling her over the edge of the cliff. In the blinding terror of those moments, she would gladly have welcomed the release.

Chapter Fourteen

The two men stood inside the small room. It was an inner chamber of some sort, its religious purpose in the monastery complex long since forgotten. Only the faded remnants of fine frescoes still lingering on the walls, despite the ravages of time, gave a hint to the Great Meteoran's former grandness. The room was so deeply insulated within the monastery that the rain could barely be heard.

Alec slowly walked around the chamber. Large boxes and crates were piled high along one wall. Against another wall stood a wide table covered with more gold, silver and priceless antiques than he had ever seen outside a museum. He looked over at Boris, who was now leaning against the wall. "Nice stuff," he said.

Boris walked to the table and picked up a large gilded silver cup. "Lovely, isn't it? They claim this is a twin to the Antioch Chalice, the one thought to have been used by Christ at the Last Supper." He smiled at Alec's bemused expression. "You still seem quite surprised that my country would want all of these things."

Alec's eyes darted to the gun in Ivanov's hand. It was a .45 autoloader. Then he shrugged. "I thought you Bolsheviks were supposed to have done away with the heirs to the Byzantine Empire, that's all."

"The tsars, you mean?"

He looked back at Boris, silently weighing his chances. "Yes."

"We did. But I want you to know, of course, that we have tried to get hold of these things through the proper channels."

Alec thought about what he knew of Ivanov. The man was an expert marksman. He had proved that on countless occasions. "Legitimate?" Alec chuckled. "What are you trying to do, justify the Crimean War to me?"

Boris was starting to grow impatient. He had lost his sense of humor. "No, I'm talking about true legal channels. We've been battling this issue in Israeli courts for years. There are millions of dollars of ecclesiastical properties in Israel alone. And we believe they are ours."

Not only was Boris an expert marksman, Alec mused, but he had spent his formative years with the KGB. Accuracy was his strong point. "You'll never win this, Ivanov."

The Russian set the chalice on the table. "No, but I will make a very big dent. I will pave the way for others to follow me. That is what we all do in the long run, is it not?"

"What if you find you are on the wrong path?"

"Any path that leads to the glorification of the state is the right one, Alec."

Alec snorted derisively. "In other words, you still believe that crap about the end justifying any course of action."

"But of course. That is why, in the long run, we will survive as a nation and you will crumble. You Americans have the fatal flaw of putting human life above all else." Boris swept his hand toward the table piled high with icons. "Your various religions have only aggravated that flaw."

"Tell me this, Ivanov. Why Janelle Lindsey?"

"Do you mean why did we involve her in this little escapade?"

"Yes, and why do you think you have to kill her? She is nothing to you."

"You are absolutely correct there. She is nothing to me." Boris waved his hand dismissively. "A mere nuisance, that is all. But, to answer your questions—first of all, she is involved because she was there. The answer to your second question is that she is now in my way. Really Alec, there is no need to look so hostile. Actually, Nikos is the one who brought her into this. Like the young fool that he was, he stole the coin from me and wanted somewhere safe to hide it. He apparently wanted to find out more about us so that he could go to the authorities with information. Now, I ask you, who better to trust it with than the naive new employee of James Eddington Bluminfeld? So you see, it was not I who involved her. It was Nikos. I simply took advantage of the situation and used her as the perfect mark for Nikos's death. It really was quite simple and quite brilliant, actually."

Alec forced every emotion except one to the back of his mind. Nothing of what he was now feeling would be allowed to surface. He had to remain calm. "Brilliant except for the coin," he said.

Ivanov's eyes flashed with irritation, but he, too, remained cool. "Hmmm, yes. Except for the coin." He scowled. "If only she had been a good girl and handed it over like I asked—none of this would have been necessary. She would have been allowed to live."

"In jail," Alec added. "As a convicted murderer."

Boris shrugged. "We all have to make our little sacrifices." He looked at Alec directly. "And now, my Western comrade, I believe that your time has come. You have asked your questions and seen what you wanted to see. In short, you have satisfied your insatiable curiosity about other people's affairs, and now you must leave."

An expert marksman, a former KGB officer, nobody's fool. "Alone?" Alec asked, smiling.

Boris didn't return the smile. "I am afraid not."

Once more Alec's gaze dropped to the .45 in Ivanov's hand. "You're not going to kill me here, then?"

Boris's eyes didn't mirror the light tone of his voice. "And soil my beautiful icons?"

"Ah," Alec said. "Of course not. How stupid of me. Okay, so where to?"

"Out."

"Out of here?"

"Yes."

Alec turned and felt the tip of the gun at his back as the two of them left the room and headed back through the dark winding corridors of the monastery. He could take a chance and try to get the gun away, but that was a wager he would probably lose. Besides, he was in no imminent danger. Boris wouldn't shoot him in the back; that would take all the fun out of it, and it really wasn't his style at all.

Outside, the rain had not slackened. The wind tried to push them back even as they forged ahead. With the gun prodding him from behind, Alec led the way down the steep sloping path they had come up earlier. It joined another path that branched off toward the front of the monastery. But they veered away from the building, down the slick, wet embankment.

As soon as they rounded the bend, Alec stopped short and the gun gouged hard into his back. With the rain streaming over their faces, both men stared down at the slumped body at their feet. Boris was instantly on guard. He grasped Alec's arm and pulled him to the side of the path. Listening for footsteps in the wet mud, they heard only the steady drill of the rain.

"She could not have done this," Boris whispered harshly. "She does not have what it takes."

Alec said nothing. But inside he was a twisted ball of live wires. One of the men who had taken Janelle was dead. But what did that mean? Was she alive? Did the other man have her somewhere? Had they hurt her...killed her...what in God's name had happened to her?

Alert now and much less confident, Boris urged Alec back onto the path with the nose of the gun. "Do not try anything, Alec Hayden, or your blood will mingle here with Sergei's." He looked down once more at the man. "No, she could not have done this."

"You underestimate her, Comrade."

"No," Boris growled. "I studied her file thoroughly. She does only what people tell her to do. She does not take action on her own. She is an unexceptional person. She would not do this."

The wind whipped the words around them, but Alec shouted over his shoulder to the Russian. "Exceptional circumstances can bring out very exceptional traits in people."

Boris said nothing. He shoved the tip of the gun against Alec's back to move him forward.

They continued along the narrow ledge that fanned out into a plateau. The wind was even stronger here in the open area, and Alec knew that this might be his best chance to go for the gun. He would have trouble keeping his bearings and his balance, but so would Ivanov. They would be on equal footing.

He shouted something over his shoulder, and Boris moved closer. "What?"

Alec shouted again. "I said that perhaps someday we will decide policy together in Hell, what do you think?"

Boris frowned. "I cannot hear..."

Alec spun around and slammed into him. The gun fired, but the bullet was directed into the wind, away from either of them. Ivanov lost his balance only temporarily, then regained it and came at Alec.

"Boris!" someone shouted from behind. "Do not move! It is over."

Boris hesitated for only one stunned moment, then jerked around and fired at the hazy figure standing twenty-five feet away in the rain. Immediately, Alec jammed his arm down hard over Ivanov's as the gun went off again. The weapon fell to the ground and Boris grabbed for it. Alec reached it first. Boris lunged at him and Alec fired once, then twice. Ivanov fell to the ground, face down in the mud, and died.

Alec's breath was coming fast, and his chest and throat ached from the cold air. He stared down at the inert body, then lifted his eyes toward the person who had fallen to the ground a few yards away. Still gripping the pistol, he bent down and pulled his Colt 380 and the gold coin from Ivanov's shirt pocket. He slipped them into his own pocket, then hurried over to the other man and knelt down, staring into the pain-distorted face.

"Voutsas! What the..."

"I am good, yes?" The minister of antiquities tried to laugh, but the sound came out as a groan. "It is only my leg."

Alec ripped back the material of Voutsas's pants leg to expose the wound. The rain pounded against it, and Alec could not tell how bad the injury really was.

Vasilos Voutsas coughed. "It is not nearly as bad as it looks." He tried to smile. "I bet you thought I wouldn't make it, didn't you?"

"I had no idea," Alec said, marveling at the man's timely appearance. "Bill Lefland called you?"

Voutsas lifted a weak arm and wiped the rain from his face. "Yes, last night. I came right away. I went to Sklavopoulos's house, then to Agios Petras. It seems I have been only a step behind you the whole way."

Alec tore a long strip of material from the pants leg and began to wrap it around the minister's thigh. "You're a good man, Voutsas. I must say, though, I never expected this."

"Where is Miss Lindsey?"

Alec sat back on his heels and frowned. He wiped his face with the sleeve of his shirt and stared into the rain. "I don't know. You saw nothing on your way up here?"

"One of Ivanov's men is lying dead at the bottom of the cliff. He must have fallen when he tried to climb to the top."

Alec looked surprised. "The other one is dead, too. He's on the pathway up there—toward the monastery. He—he was stabbed."

"By Miss Lindsey?" Voutsas's face expressed the same surprise that Alec had felt.

"I don't know."

The minister coughed in pain once again and closed his eyes. "But if they are both dead, then she must be all right, yes?"

Alec scowled down at the gun he had dropped beside the minister's body. He shook his head. "Something doesn't click. I don't know what it is, but something... I've got to find her. Come on, let's get you someplace dry."

"No, please do not worry about my leg. Go find the woman. I will tag along."

"No," Alec said, standing up. He bent over and drew Voutsas gently upward. The man's injured leg hung useless above the ground. "I won't leave you here. Come on." He slipped Ivanov's gun into his jeans pocket and put the one Voutsas had used back into his coat pocket. Wrapping one arm around the minister's waist and looping the man's arm over his shoulder, Alec led him slowly across the field of scrub pine toward the pathway that led up to the Great Meteoran.

"I do not think we have anyone else to worry about," Voutsas said as he limped along beside Alec.

"I hope you're right."

"I'm sure of it. Bluminfeld is in Athens. He has no idea that we have uncovered his operation. Everyone else who mattered is dead."

"She thinks I'm involved," Alec said, struggling to help the minister walk through the driving rain.

"Who?"

"Miss Lindsey. She thinks I betrayed her. She thinks I am in with Boris."

"Ah," said Voutsas, trying to keep his balance. "Then she may be—unpredictable."

"Highly."

"And dangerous."

Alec was silent. It was too much of an effort to talk and help Voutsas along the narrow ledge that rounded the cliff. Besides, he didn't know what he thought at this point. If Janelle was still alive, she was angry and probably scared out of her mind. He didn't want to think too far ahead. All he wanted to believe was that she was alive and that she had not been hurt by Ivanov's underlings. That was all he dared hope for.

The two men worked their way slowly up the steep path, past the body that lay slumped in the mud, and on up to the monastery at the top of the rock mountain. Once they were inside, Alec eased Voutsas to the floor in a corner, where he could lean back against the wall.

Alec reached into his pocket and pulled out the gold coin. He held it out to Voutsas. "You're sure you'll be okay?"

The minister smiled and took the coin from Alec's hand. "Yes, I am sure. Now go find your Miss Lindsey. Go, please."

Alec hesitated, wondering in which direction he should go first. He would go back to the path, and if the rain had not washed away her footprints, he would follow wherever they would lead. From the doorway, he glanced back once at Vasilos Voutsas, then hurried out into the rain in search of Janelle.

Chapter Fifteen

Janelle crouched in the dark corridor of the monastery. She could hear the voices in the entry hall, but she couldn't make out everything they were saying. She heard Alec say something about going to look for her. She pressed back farther against the wall, hoping that if he came this way, he would not see her. He was a part of this. He was in on the operation with Boris. Boris wanted to kill her. Alec would probably...

She squeezed her eyes shut and buried her face in her hands to keep from crying out. No! It wasn't true. It couldn't be. Alec would not kill her. He was not that type of man. He had been the one who had protected her, fed her, clothed her... made love to her. She wasn't sure what his part in all of this was, but she knew beyond a shadow of a doubt that he was no murderer. He could not have been that good a liar. She meant something to him, she just knew it. She would not accept that it had all been a lie. Alec was not Nikos. And he was definitely not a killer.

It was she who was the murderer.

She choked back the cry that wanted to come out. She had killed a man. With her own hands, she had taken another life. And in this moment, it didn't seem to matter that he would have killed her first if he had been given the opportunity. All that was clear was that she had killed him. She was a murderer.

Oh, Alec—where was he? She was scared. She was alone. There was no one she could turn to. If—just supposing he was a criminal, if he had been in on the deal with Boris to get the coin from her...she had to find out on her own. She had to find the treasures, contact the authorities in Athens and whoever was clean would surface to the top. If Alec wasn't involved, she would know it then. For now, she was going to stay out of his path. It was the only safe place to be.

She listened for the sound of voices, but she no longer heard them. Either they had left the monastery or they were waiting in some trap they had set for her. She would not fall into it. She would go in the opposite direction until she found where they had hidden the treasures.

As quietly as possible, she stood up. The wind blew a door shut nearby, and she pressed back against the wall, praying that no one had heard. Slowly she eased herself down the hallway, angling around the corners when the corridor twisted and turned, feeling her way inch by inch along the cold, damp stones of the walls.

VASILOS VOUTSAS FROWNED at the loud sound. A door, somewhere inside the monastery, had slammed shut. Most likely, it was only the wind. But perhaps it was something more. He shifted his weight and tried to straighten out his leg. It hurt like mad to move it. Although he didn't believe that the bullet had penetrated any bone, he knew he would need medical treatment soon. He shivered inside his soaked cloth-

ing and stared out the open doorway, wondering
which way Alec had gone.

He looked again toward the hallway that led back
into the bowels of the monastery. The sound of the
door had come from there. And it made him wonder.
He rested his head against the wall and closed his eyes.
All he could do now was wait for Alec to come back.
Then he would tell him about the noise. If he didn't
come back this way... Voutsas tried to straighten the
leg again, but the pain was too severe. He wasn't at all
sure what he would do if Alec did not come back this
way.

JANELLE STOOD IN THE DOORWAY of the room and
stared at the rich display of gold and silver and bronze.
Light from butane lamps hanging on the walls reflected off the precious metals and bathed the room in
a golden glow. A table was piled high with goblets and
bowls and statues, candelabras and paintings. At one
end of the table was folded an intricate tapestry, em-
broidered in gold and silver thread. Propped up
against the wall was an altarpiece of solid gold, with
precious gems laid out in a design of prophets, saints
and angels. Next to it was a carved wooden scene, de-
picting the birth of Christ. She thought of Father
Gregouriou, an old, tired monk in a black robe and
cylindrical hat, who had spent his life carving such
scenes in a small room high in the forbidding mountains of Greece. Her eyes swept across the table.
Where had all these treasures come from? How many
churches, monasteries and private collections had been
violated in the accumulation of this incredible store-
house of wealth?

Shivering, she slipped off her sweater and tried to wring out some of the water. She was stalling, she knew. For now that she had found the proof, now that she knew where it was hidden and who was involved, she must somehow make her way back to Kalambaka and call the police. She would have to lead them back up here. She would have to show them the stolen relics. She would have to show them the bodies. And she would have to name names. How much could she tell them? Would she be able to turn Alec over to the police? She loved him. No matter what he had done, she knew that she loved him. He had let her inside his life; he had confided in her. She had told him about her parents, about her feelings for Nikos. They had shared more than their bodies with each other; they had shared the secrets of their souls. Could she allow him to be locked behind the same bars he had risked his career to help her escape?

She draped her sweater over her arm and closed her eyes, praying that she would wake up and find that this had all been a dream, a nightmare that seemed to have no end. Her eyes flew open and her body froze as she heard a sound moving down the corridor. It was the squish of wet boots, and it was coming closer, heading this way. Boris? Alec? Both had no doubt been soaked by the heavy rain. But then, Alec hadn't worn boots. Boris had not been wearing boots, either.

The sound stopped for a moment and then started up again. Squish, squish... There was a familiarity to the sound, something that tripped a funny little switch inside her head. A squish of boots, a hot afternoon on the dry hillside of Karpathos, a dark shadow that fell across her path....

As a clear remembrance of the sound struck her, Janelle turned and stared at the rain-soaked figure now standing in the doorway of the room.

Her mouth opened to speak, but no sound came out. She tried again as the man walked into the room, but the words she wanted to say were just not there.

He lifted his hand and brushed at the dark wet hair that hung in his face. "Well, *mou* Jani, you have come much farther than I would have believed possible. How is it that you have not died yet?"

Janelle stared as if she were seeing a ghost. Her mouth, she knew, was hanging open, but she couldn't make it respond to her command to close it. "You— you are dead," she said, realizing the moment the words were out how stupid they sounded even to her. "I thought—you were dead."

"Am I dead, Jani? Perhaps in this moment, you are only hallucinating. Perhaps I am not really here at all."

She frowned, wondering the same thing. Nothing made sense anymore. Nothing was as it appeared. She wondered vaguely if she was losing her mind. "They said—they said your body had washed up on the rocks of Karpathos—that day we met."

He smiled, revealing his crooked teeth. "If that was so, then how could I have been watching you earlier today from the bushes?"

"You?"

"Yes. I thought at one point that you had seen me, but I guess I was wrong. How fortunate for me."

Her body was on autopilot, her mouth moving on its own. "Then whose body was it that washed up?"

"Some person with the Ministry of Antiquities."

"Mavro Sklavopoulos?"

He shrugged. "I suppose that was his name...yes, that was it. Boris sent him to find me. I found him first."

Her blood froze in her veins as the thought came to her. "Your boots were wet that day...as they are now. You—you had been down at the water, hadn't you? Just before you came up to meet with me."

"That is correct."

Her eyes lowered to the knife in his hand, and she lifted her startled gaze back up to his face.

He smiled. "You are confused, yes?"

She nodded slowly, a frown of bewilderment distorting her features. "Yes. I—I don't understand, Zafer. I...why did you lie to me...about your relationship with Nikos, about the family treasures, about...everything?"

"Because, *mou* Jani, I had to." He stepped farther into the room, and she instinctively stepped back. He smiled at her reaction as if it amused him greatly. Leaning against the wall, he ran the tip of the knife blade beneath his fingernails to clean them. "If I had told you that I was helping a Russian authority—no, what is the word?—ah, diplomat, and an American diplomat...if I had told you that we were stealing these antiquities and then smuggling them to the Soviet Union, what would you have said?" He shrugged his shoulders. "So you see, Jani, I could not tell the truth to you, yes?"

Janelle shook her head in disbelief. Not one person had told her the truth about anything. It had all been lies. Everything. From the first moment she had come to Greece, she had been drenched in dishonesty and deception. Was everything she had learned about Nikos a lie, too?

"How did Nikos get the coin?"

Zafer seemed to like that question. "Boris had cre-ated in Nikos a master thief. How was he to know that his pupil would use the same learned techniques on the teacher? In Nikos, Boris created a—a monstèr, I be-lieve you call it."

The sweater dropped from Janelle's arm, and she bent over to pick it up. She stood up without it. What was the point? "And his death? You told me that Bo-ris killed—that..." Janelle stopped and swallowed hard. She stared at Zafer. He was shaking his head. "You lied to me—about that, too?"

"Yes."

She hesitated, not at all sure that she wanted to delve any further. The question came anyway. "Then..."

Zafer smiled his crooked smile and ran his finger along the edge of the knife blade.

A nonsensical childhood verse began to play in her head. "You?" There was a crooked man who walked a crooked mile... smiled a crooked smile...

"Yes."

This wasn't happening. She wasn't standing here talking to Nikos's murderer. Boris, yes. The two Rus-sians who had planned to kill her, yes. But Zafer? The man who had made her feel so welcome when she first arrived in his country? "Why?" she asked, not knowing what else to say.

Zafer was enjoying himself immensely. "Why? Well, you see, it is because I was paid a great deal of money to kill him."

Paid to kill. Somehow that had never occurred to her. She had never thought that she might know someone who was paid to kill. "By whom?"

"Who paid me?"

"Yes."

He shrugged. "Boris and . . . oh, you will like this. Your chargé d'affaires."

"Bluminfeld?"

"That is the one."

"James Bluminfeld hired you to kill Nikos? I don't believe you!" It was impossible. He might be involved in the smuggling operation. He might want the priceless coin for his collection. And he might even take money from a Russian agent, if the price was right. But...murder? She had worked for him. If only for a week, she had sat in the small office next to his. She had discussed staff problems, she had helped him plan dinner parties for visiting dignitaries, she had gone over agendas for meetings. If he was a murderer, wouldn't she have known it?

Nothing was as it seemed.

Her heart pounded loudly in her chest. She didn't want to ask. She didn't want to know.

Yes, she did want to know. "And Alec?" she asked softly. "What is his part in all of this?" She didn't even breathe while she waited for Zafer's answer.

He looked disconcerted for the first time. "Alec? I know no Alec. Who is he?"

The breath escaped from her lungs in one long sigh. He didn't know Alec. That could only mean that whatever part Alec played, it must be minimal. It was too much for her to hope that maybe he had actually been telling her the truth all along. No one, it seemed, did that anymore.

She watched Zafer shift his weight to the other foot and lean back once more against the wall. The bewildered expression was gone from her face. Now there was only sadness. "I thought you were Nikos's friend, Zafer."

"I was. That was why I was the one to do it."

She shook her head. "So you followed him to my house?"

"No. I told him I would help him go to the police. I told him that you, Jani, would help us. I told him that we must meet with you at your house."

"So you led him to his own murder."

Zafer just shrugged and went back to cleaning his fingernails.

"And the note?" she asked. "The one that was written to me? The one clutched in his hand?"

He smiled, genuinely pleased with himself, and his crooked teeth gleamed gold in the glow of the lamps. "I wrote that. I handed it to him. And then, when he died, it remained clutched in his fist."

All she wanted to do right now was find a corner where she could curl up and go to sleep. She didn't want to keep asking these questions. She wished she could just close her mind to the whole ugly business. "Why did you want it?" she heard herself ask.

"The coin?"

"Yes."

"Because with that, I would have more power with Boris. He would be forced to pay me more money. Your chargé wanted it, and without it, he would not help with the shipping of the cargo. So you see, Boris would have paid me a great deal of money to get the coin."

"I never once suspected you, Zafer. Never once."

"That is good. That is the way I hoped it would be." He cocked his head and smiled gently at her. "And now, Jani, you will go quietly, yes?"

Her eyes were riveted on his face. Slowly she lowered them again to the knife that was now clutched tightly in his grip.

"You will not cause problems," he said, his voice almost soothing.

"Problems?" she repeated, still not comprehending what was happening.

"Yes." He smiled. "It will make no difference, you know. You will die one way or another. You can go quickly. I can make sure of that. Or you can die very, very slowly. It is entirely up to you."

The pounding of her heart moved up to her neck. She tasted something bitter in the back of her throat. She had made it so far. She had fought everyone to live as long as she had. It was inconceivable that she would die now. "I don't want to die."

"But you must. It is your time."

She shook her head, denying it. No, Zafer Demir was wrong. It was not her time to die. She would not accommodate him.

She glanced sideways at the table covered with priceless antiques, and without another thought, she reached for the silver chalice and hurled it across the room.

Zafer raised his arm, and the chalice glanced off him, falling with a loud clang to the floor. He stood still, surprised by her sudden action.

She reached for a bronze candle holder and flung it at him. Again he covered his face, and the object merely grazed the back of his hand.

The next item came faster. She was picking up things as fast as she could, throwing them without even bothering to aim. He tried to dodge all of the blows, but one of the goblets struck him hard on the side of his head. She saw the blood drip down from his temple.

But nothing she threw stopped him. He kept moving toward her. She was backed farther and farther into the corner. She had nowhere else to go.

He raised the knife to charge at her and plunge it into her body, and she knew she was trapped.

She screamed.

At that moment something leaped across the room from the doorway and landed on top of Zafer. The knife shot from his hand and skidded across the floor, stopping at Janelle's feet. Her hands were pressed flat against the wall, and her throat was dry from screaming. She stared at the two men wrestling about on the floor.

Alec and Zafer. Rolling over and over, one fist flying into another's face, knees kicked hard into stomachs. Painful groans and angry curses. She tried to keep up with what was happening, but everything changed so fast. Only a moment ago, Alec had knocked Zafer across the room, but now Zafer was on top of him, his large hands clutched around Alec's throat.

Janelle stooped down and picked up the knife. She shifted it from hand to hand. Her head throbbed, and every muscle in her body was clenched in anticipation. Could she do it? Could she walk over to Zafer and kill him? That afternoon she had killed a man, but it had been an accident. He had come after her, tried to kill her. This was different. This would be premeditated.

Alec's hands were clenched around Zafer's forearms, his muscles straining to push Demir away.

She had to do it. She had to save Alec's life.

She took a step forward and gripped the knife tightly in her right hand. A cry of fear came from her throat. She took another step forward, but at that moment Alec strained hard and shoved Zafer off him. He leaned forward, gasping for breath as Zafer lunged at him again.

A gunshot splintered the air and reverberated through the cavernous rooms and the winding corridors of the crumbling monastery, bounding off every wall in the small room. Janelle screamed and slumped down in the corner, her eyes clamped shut to hide from whatever terror still awaited her.

There was only silence. The room was empty of echoes, the corridors hauntingly quiet.

Janelle opened her eyes. Zafer was lying in the far corner, not moving. Alec was sitting against the far wall, breathing heavily.

Janelle looked at the doorway. A man she had never seen before was down on one knee, his leg stuck out at an odd angle, a piece of cloth from his pants wrapped crudely around his upper thigh. His face was drawn and pale, and in his hand was the gun that had killed Zafer Demir.

Janelle glanced down at her own hand, realizing for the first time that she still held the knife. She slowly opened her fingers, and it fell to the floor with a ping.

She looked over at Alec. He was trying to stand up, so she quickly rose and went over to help him. After she had got him to his feet, he leaned back weakly against the wall. His jaw and neck were bruised, and there was a small split in his lip.

She stared up at him, unable to speak, unable to formulate the words that would describe what she was feeling. With a strength that surprised them both, he wrapped his arms around her and pulled her roughly against him. Her head was pressed against his chest, and she could hear the rapid pounding of his heart.

As quickly as he had grabbed her, he released her. His eyes left her face and moved to the man in the doorway. He stepped away from the wall and knelt down beside him, lifted him upright and brought him into the room, then propped him up against the wall. The man smiled weakly.

Alec shook his head. "Dammit, Voutsas!" he exclaimed, his voice hoarse and dry. "You've got the best damn timing I've ever seen!"

The minister tried to laugh, but it was a feeble attempt. "I thought—" He coughed and grimaced in pain. "I thought you Americans were supposed to know how to fight. Didn't you learn anything from watching all those cowboy movies on your television?"

Alec checked the wound on Voutsas's leg. "My mother didn't believe in television. We never owned one."

"A pity," Voutsas sputtered.

Janelle knelt down beside Alec and moved her bewildered eyes from one face to the other.

Alec smiled at her. "Janelle, I want you to meet Vasilos Voutsas, minister of antiquities and restoration. This is Miss Lindsey."

The minister reached out his hand, but it immediately fell limp to his side. "I am honored, Miss Lindsey. But . . . I seem to have used up all of my energy."

She stared at the man in awe. "You must rest."

Alec turned to her and spoke hoarsely. "He has no energy because twice today he has saved my life." He turned back to Voutsas. "I owe you a great deal."

The man shook his head. "You have done a great deal. If not for you and Miss Lindsey, we would never have recovered these items..." He glanced around at the relics that lay broken and shattered about the room. He shrugged. "That is, what is left of them." He looked back at the two of them. "Without you, we would never have known who was behind it."

Alec patted his shoulder. "Rest now, Voutsas. We'll try to get help."

"Can we get him to a hospital?" Janelle asked, all thoughts of what she had been through on hold until this more immediate problem was solved.

Voutsas lifted his hand to interrupt. It fell back to the floor. "I called the authorities from Kalambaka. I explained the situation before I came up here. I told them to expect injuries and to have reinforcements brought in." He smiled at their expressions. "In Greece, the wheels turn very slowly."

Alec laughed. "So we've heard. Well, come on. We'll help you down the mountain to the road. Maybe your reinforcements stopped there to have a picnic." He looked at Janelle. "Are you all right?"

It was a question too deep and too painful for her even to consider right now, but she knew what Alec wanted to know. "Yes, I can help. Just tell me what to do."

Alec stood up and pulled Voutsas to his feet, balancing him until Janelle could get on his other side. "Just let him rest his arm across your shoulder," Alec instructed. "And put your arm around his waist. Try to prop up his weight. I'll do the same on this side."

With Vasilos between them, his weight resting on their shoulders, they led him out of the room and along the winding corridors. None of them had given a second glance at the inert body that lay amid the jumble of priceless Byzantine relics.

They lef the Great Meteoran and headed down the pa hway that would eventually take them to the main road. The rain had almost stopped, and now only misty clouds blew across the mountaintops. The three people did not pause in their careful trek through the rocky cliffs. Janelle and Alec concentrated only on getting Vasilos Voutsas, the man who had saved their lives, safely down the mountain.

Chapter Sixteen

Janelle stood on the sidewalk in Kalambaka and watched the two attendants close the rear door of the ambulance and climb into the front seat. Then the vehicle slowly pulled away from the curb. Vasilos Voutsas would be taken to the nearest hospital for treatment and would most likely rest there for a couple of days before being transported back to Athens. She watched listlessly until the ambulance had disappeared around the corner.

Alec was standing in the middle of the street, talking with the Greek gendarmerie. One side of his face was bruised and swollen, but the cut in his lip didn't seem to be bothering him. The inspector from police headquarters in Athens was there, also, and he kept glancing over at Janelle as if he was afraid she would run at any minute.

A helicopter sat in the field across the street, its blade whirring impatiently. The pilot was waiting to take the inspector, Alec and Janelle back to Athens. They would be detained; Alec had already told her to expect that. There would be questions to answer, reports to fill out, red tape to unwind.

She looked up at the sky. Here in Kalambaka it was clear, with the sun hovering just above the western horizon. It would be a beautiful evening. She could hardly believe that she and Alec had left for the mountains only that morning and that, considering what had happened, only one day had passed. Only one day, and yet she had lived a lifetime during it.

She felt very old.

Her eyes lifted to the sharp, rocky pinnacles. A few low-lying clouds still hung over the peaks of some of the mountains. Above them, the sky was blue. It would be a beautiful night up on those forbidding mountaintop retreats.

Alec walked over to where she was standing on the sidewalk. "They're going to go up and retrieve the bodies and the relics."

Her voice, when she spoke, was empty. "And Bluminfeld?"

"He'll be taken into custody."

She glanced up at the twisted pillars of stone, skirted by graceful olive groves and orchards of almond and peach. A thin gray cloud swept over the tip of one of the rock needles. She watched it almost absently, wondering at the emptiness she felt inside. "Those mountains were supposed to be a retreat from the world's violence."

Alec studied her brittle expression. Her mouth was drawn thin and tight, and her eyes were listless and cloudy. Her clothes were torn and stiff from the rain and mud. Her neck and arms were covered with scratches. Fatigue hovered over her, weighing her down. "Are you ready to go?"

She nodded with a sigh and allowed him to take her arm and lead her across the street and onto the field where the chopper waited. The wind from the blades whipped at their clothes and hair as they climbed aboard. Janelle sat in front next to the pilot; Alec sat in back beside the inspector. Obviously the interrogation process would begin before they made it back to Athens.

As soon as they were buckled in, the helicopter lifted off the ground, skimming the treetops and the mountains as it angled southeast over the Thessalian plains toward the coast.

Janelle closed her eyes and, lulled by the low Greek sounds of the conversation in the back seat, drifted into a light sleep. Even after they had landed in Athens and were driving to police headquarters, Janelle remained in a kind of hypnotized stupor. She could feel nothing. She wondered if she ever would again.

Once inside the station, she was led to a room and seated at a long table. Alec sat at one end, the inspector next to him. Two other policemen she had never seen before stood leaning against the wall. An American in a three-piece suit walked into the room and closed the door.

He glanced over at Alec. "Well, Hayden, I see you're trying to play Dirty Harry again."

Alec chuckled wearily. "No, I have to hand that role over to Vasilos Voutsas. That man can wield a gun with the best of them."

The American smiled and looked at Janelle. "You must be Miss Lindsey."

"Yes."

He held out his hand. "I'm Perkins. I work with Alec at the State Department. When we heard what was going on here, we thought maybe you two could use a little help."

Aren't you a little late? she wanted to say, but instead she met his hand with her own and said nothing.

Perkins turned toward the inspector and spoke in Greek. Then he looked at Alec and Janelle. "There are still some questions." His expression was apologetic. "I'll try to hurry him up."

Alec shook his head. "Take your time, Perkins. I want to get this over with once and for all. I don't want anything hanging over our heads. And when I leave this building, I don't want to come back."

Perkins nodded. "I know how you hate loose ends, Hayden. Well, okay, here goes."

The inspector opened a file in front of him and began asking one question after another, which Perkins did his best to translate.

"I would like Miss Lindsey to clarify her relationship with the deceased Nikos Marinatos."

Janelle clasped her hands in front of her on the table and stared at her jagged nails. She was a mess. Her hair was matted against her head, and her clothes were filthy and torn. "We were acquaintances, nothing more."

"And how long have you know James Eddington Bluminfeld?"

"We met a little over a week ago when I came to Greece to work for the American government."

"And he showed you a collection of rare coins on that first day?"

"Yes."

"Did he ever mention this other one . . . this Byzantine coin of Constantine?"

"No."

"And you, Alec, you had reason to suspect that an official of the American embassy in Athens was involved in a smuggling operation with the Russian embassy?"

"The United States Department of State had been contacted by a man..."

Janelle clasped her hands tightly together and tried to force out the sounds of the men's voices around her. She didn't want to hear anymore about it. She didn't want to think about it. She just wanted to go away. She wanted to take a shower. She wanted peace.... "I'm sorry?" She glanced up when she finally realized that Perkins was speaking to her.

"The inspector wants to know how the two men who held you captive on the mountain died."

Janelle stared at him, and her heart began to pound rapidly in her chest and throat. "I—I was running away from them. They were going to kill me. I climbed the cliff, and one of the men was unable to climb up behind me. He must have...the wind must have blown him off the cliff."

"And the other?"

She glanced at Alec. His mouth curved upward in a gentle, encouraging smile. She looked back at Perkins and tried to swallow the memory that formed a clot at the back of her throat. "He threw a knife at me. I—I picked it up and then...he came at me. I didn't mean to...it..."

Alec interrupted then and finished what Janelle could not say. She looked at him gratefully. Even now he was protecting her, shielding her from the pain. She had been so wrong to believe that he could have been involved with Ivanov and Bluminfeld. She had been so wrong to doubt him.

"And the man who was killed by Vasilos Voutsas, the man called Zafer Demir . . . was this the same man you saw on the island of Karpathos?"

"Yes."

The questions kept coming, one after another, and the hours seemed to drag around her. The inspector and the two other policemen were frantically making notes, stopping now and then to compare them or to talk among themselves. Then would come still another question, another loose end that had to be tied up. She knew that the biggest snag—and the hardest aspect for the inspector to accept about this whole situation—was the fact that she had escaped from his custody. He had placed her under arrest, and she had fled. It took the most persuasive arguments and almost all of the energy from both Perkins and Alec, as well as the specter of the American government hovering in the background, to convince the inspector that Janelle should not be charged with the crime of resisting arrest.

Finally, after what seemed like days, the inspector stood up, said something in Greek to Perkins and Alec, nodded solemnly to Janelle and then left the room, flanked by the two other officers.

Only Janelle, Perkins and Alec were left in the silent wake, drained and exhausted from the long interrogation. After several uncomfortable seconds, Perkins slapped his hands together and beamed. "Well, that's that. Shall we all go get good 'n' drunk?"

Janelle's eyes were directed to her clasped hands on the table. Alec's eyes were riveted on her face. Without looking at Perkins, he said, "You go ahead. We may join you later at the hotel."

"Oh...." Perkins looked from one to the other and cleared his throat. "Okay. Nobody can accuse me of not being able to take a hint." When he got no response to his little joke, he cleared his throat again and gathered up his papers. "I got us reservations at the Caravel." He tossed a hotel-room key to Alec, then slipped out, closing the door behind him.

The silence in the small room was palpable. "Well," Janelle finally said. "You certainly do have a lot of clout, don't you? I mean, if I didn't have you around, I'd be working on some chain gang by now or making license plates or something."

He ignored her cynical tone, realizing that it had been born from too much pain, too much fear and far too much reality. A person could take just so much. He wanted to touch her, but he was afraid of what might happen. Would she lash out at him? Would she cry and let him comfort her? Or would she break? The first two, he could handle. But if she shattered, he would never forgive himself.

He stood up and walked over to her, leaning on the table in front of her. His hands grasped the edge of the table. "Your faith in human nature has been stretched to the limit, hasn't it?"

She held her hands stiffly in her lap and wouldn't look at him. "I—I killed a man up there today."

God, if he could just touch her. If he could just somehow make the pain go away from her eyes. "That was self-defense, Janelle. There's a big difference."

She looked dubious. "I might have killed Zafer when he was trying to strangle you. That wouldn't have been self-defense."

"That's called saving the good guy."

She glanced up and saw the tentative smile that played around his lips. He was trying so hard, even though he too had been through hell. His shirt was ripped at one shoulder, and flecks of dried blood dotted the front. "I thought for a while that you weren't one of the good guys."

"I know. I'll never forget the look on your face." His face grew still, his mouth tense. "I'd do anything in the world not to have you look at me like that again. I would never hurt you, Janelle. I want you to know that. And believe that."

She took note of the pained expression on his face, but she couldn't get past her own doubts and anxieties. "You were so friendly to Boris."

"I was trying to buy us some time."

She wanted to reach out and touch the bruise on the left side of his face, to somehow make his hurt go away, too. "There were several times up there on the mountain when my time almost ran out. There—there were moments when I would almost have welcomed it."

"But you didn't, Janelle." He laid his hand against the side of her face, forcing her to look at him. "You could have caved in, but you didn't."

Her eyes were moist, and the sadness in her voice tore a hole in his heart. "I'm not so sure, Alec."

His thumb stroked a gentle path along her cheekbone, making her want to drown in the sensations of his touch. Could he banish the pain? Together could they find the peace they so desperately needed?

"They all thought I wasn't capable, didn't they, Alec?"

He reached out with both hands and pulled her to her feet. With one hand at her lower back, he guided her to him until their bodies were almost touching. His other hand was against her face, and his thumb moved over her lips. "They were wrong, Janelle. They were all wrong. You're the most capable woman I know. Your life has value, meaning...even if they didn't know that, you did. That's what kept you going. That's what kept you fighting to stay alive."

"Everyone was so full of lies," she said, and a single tear slid down her cheek. Alec gently wiped it away. "I never doubted what people told me before. I never knew the world was so full of deceit."

"The whole world isn't, Janelle. Don't let this ordeal harden you into thinking that. That's what has happened to me over the years. I started believing there was no such thing as truth, or goodness, or—" he smiled at her "—innocence. I realize now how wrong I was. It may take you awhile to wring all the lies from your soul, but you will." He put his hand behind her head and combed his fingers through her tangled hair. "I'll help you, Janelle. We'll help each other."

Her hands lifted tentatively to his arms and slid slowly up over the sleeves of his shirt. "You were the only one, Alec...out of all the people who lied to me, you weren't one of them. All along, you were truthful." She searched deeply into the gray mist of his eyes. "Why?"

He hesitated while his gaze dropped to her mouth and then lifted back to her eyes. "Because I love you, Janelle. It took me awhile to figure that out. But I think I fell in love with you the first time I saw you, here in police headquarters...not exactly the most romantic setting, I agree, but I don't know...when I saw those deep brown eyes of yours and listened to you talk...."

"You could have fooled me," she said, smiling wistfully. "I thought you wanted me to get life imprisonment. You looked at me as if I were so—I don't know, so unworthy."

Alec pulled her close and rested his chin on the top of her head. "I never meant to do that. It's a habit, I guess. I have to presume guilt with some people and..." His mouth dropped to the side of her neck and then moved in a slow trail up her jaw. "If anyone is unworthy, it's me." He looked at her then, his eyes very serious, very deep. "You're so good, Janelle. And I've seen and done so much."

"Maybe you'll tell me about it someday," she said softly.

He shifted both hands to the back of her hips and pulled her closer. "Whatever you want to know."

"You want to know a secret?" she whispered, her face only inches from his.

He couldn't resist the urge to kiss the corner of her mouth. "Sure."

"Even when I thought you might be involved with Boris and the smuggling operation, I knew I would never have been able to turn you in to the police. Not the man who had believed in me, protected me...made love to me the way you did."

He tightened his grip on her, and his voice grew hoarse. "I thought I had lost you up there today. I was afraid. I don't ever want to lose you, Janelle."

She smiled up at him. "You won't, Alec. You're stuck with me, remember?"

His voice, when he spoke, was dry and husky. "Let's get out of here, before I get us both arrested for inappropriate sexual conduct in a public place."

He wrapped his arm around her shoulder and led her through the building and out onto the warm, dark sidewalk. It was nighttime in Greece, a time for lovers to stroll arm in arm past the tavernas, a time for celebration and music and wine.

"You know, Alec," she said as they walked together toward the hotel, "until just a short time ago, life was so uneventful. There was always activity in the diplomatic circles where I was growing up. I mean, we went and did and saw. But I realize now that those were all events that surrounded my father. They had nothing to do with me or with what I want out of my life. I just tagged along, invisible in his shadow."

"And now?"

"I don't know. Now, I feel...changed somehow. I have to learn how to put my work in its proper perspective. It has always been the only thing I had going for me. Planning a career in the diplomatic corps was what won my parents' approval. I thought it was what I wanted."

"The only approval you need is your own, Janelle."

She put her arm around his waist. "I know that now. But it's certainly going to be a different way of looking at things."

"Yeah," he murmured. "For me, too."

She glanced up quickly at his profile, illuminated by the glow from a streetlamp. "What do you mean?"

"My job has always been the most important thing in my life. I think it was so important because it was all I had. All of my energy and time and . . . well, my whole life has gone into it.''

"How long have you been divorced, Alec?"

"Eight years. I was still a field agent for the FBI in Atlanta when we were married. Erin didn't handle the job well. No, maybe that's unfair. Maybe I'm the one who handled it badly. I wanted to get ahead in my career, and I never felt any great fulfillment from my marriage to her . . . so I let the job sweep me away and she let . . . well . . ." He looked down at Janelle and kissed her temple, tightening his arm around her shoulder.

The night was balmy, the air filled with the fragrance of spring. Funny, but Janelle didn't even notice the smells of sulfur and exhaust in the air. Everything looked and tasted and smelled like Heaven.

They reached the hotel and took the elevator to the tenth floor. At the door to their room, Janelle reached out to touch his arm.

"We've got quite a few things to work out, don't we, Alec. Lots of ghosts to leave behind."

He had unlocked the door and pushed it open, but he stopped now to look at her closely. His arms came around her, and he drew her up in front of him. "It will be like starting over, Janelle. For both of us."

"Just the two of us," she said, clasping her hands behind his neck.

"Yes. Just you and me. Out from the shadows of your father and out from those of Erin."

"And what about the past week? Will we be able to leave what has happened behind?"

"We'll put it where it belongs, Janelle. That's all we can do. We'll move ahead and—and I promise you that we'll make it good for each other."

She smiled and ran the tip of one finger along the outline of his mouth. "It will be good, won't it?"

"I can guarantee it."

"And...we'll go first to that warm beach where we can be all alone? Where we can get to know each other?"

His hand dropped to the top of her blouse, and his finger slid in a slow trail down the buttons. "Yes," he breathed huskily. "We'll melt together under the sun."

Her heartbeat accelerated as images of them together formed in her mind. She whispered breathlessly, "I wish we were there now."

His slow smile washed over her, and the pulse began to pound in her neck. "We are, Janelle. We just don't have the sun. But we don't need it. We can start the melting process right now. Tonight."

As their eyes locked together, she had trouble getting the words out of her constricted throat. "It's what I want, too, Alec. It's all I ever want."

He pulled her into the room and slammed the door shut behind them. His mouth came down on hers, and he lovingly drank her in, sip by sip. "Then melt," he moaned against her parted lips. "Melt into me now."

They came together then, their hearts beating as one, full of joy, full of high spirits. Full of *kefi*.

Epilogue

Janelle stood mesmerized in front of the large rose-wood desk in Bluminfeld's office. Alec was standing on one side of her, Frank Osborn on the other. They were all staring at the large teak case that was open before them.

Frank counted the rows of coins. "Forty five of 'em. Pretty impressive, isn't it?"

Janelle reached out to touch a bronze Roman coin. The label below the coin dated it at 220 A.D. "I wonder where he got them all," she marveled.

Frank shook his head. "Makes you wonder how many lives were lost for each of these." She stepped back and he closed the case. "I understand Voutsas is going to display the Constantine coin in the museum."

"That's what we heard," Alec said, then chuckled. "He said he might stand beside it on crutches, just to show people what it sometimes takes to procure these museum exhibits."

Frank laughed. "At least the old boy's got a sense of humor. He's a tough cookie, isn't he?"

"He is at that."

"Hmm, I may have to keep an eye on him."

"Yes," Janelle murmured dryly. "You never know when someone's going to come up right behind you. Isn't that so, Frank?"

He grinned sheepishly, then shuffled his feet. "Hey, Janelle, I didn't mean to scare you that day. I guess I could use one of those courses in winning friends and influencing people, couldn't I?"

"It's called tact," Alec said, smiling.

"Well, how's this for tact? Where the hell is my Retsina you promised me?"

"On your desk. A whole case of it. If you'd ever get to work, you'd find it."

"Good. I was sure looking for an excuse to get drunk this afternoon. What can I drink to?"

Janelle smiled. "Us going away."

"Where are you heading?"

Janelle looked at Alec, then back at Frank. "To Tunisia. Alec insists the beaches there are great. We haven't had enough ruins, so we're going to go lie under those of Carthage."

"We're going to melt," Alec added with a quick wink at Janelle.

"Well," said Frank, oblivious to the sensual undercurrents that flowed from Alec to Janelle and back again. "They're uncrowded, that's for sure. Real private. But then, I guess that's what you two are looking for, isn't it?"

Alec wrapped his arm around Janelle's shoulder. "I've got to hand it to you, Frank. You are one smart Texan."

Frank watched them turn and walk arm in arm toward the door. The light from the hallway cast a single shadow of the two of them across the floor of

Bluminfeld's office. "You're leaving right now?" he asked, surprised.

They stopped and stared at him. "Yes, Frank. We're leaving right now. The limo is waiting to take us to the airport."

"Oh," he said, scratching his head as if he couldn't quite figure it out. "Well, heck, okay. I guess it's okay."

Alec and Janelle laughed at that. "Thanks, old buddy," Alec said. "I'm sure glad you approve."

"Of course I approve. Why wouldn't I? You two are about the best I've seen in a long time. And I just want to say—well, if it makes any difference, Janelle, you would have been a great member of our team."

She smiled at him. "Thank you, Frank. I really mean that. I would have enjoyed working with you, too."

"Yeah," he said, "you'll probably make one hell of an ambassador someday. Just like your old man."

Janelle grinned and looked up at Alec. "Foreign service . . ." She shrugged. "It's not all it's cracked up to be." She looked back at the head of security. "No, Frank, I think I'd like to find a job with some excitement for a change. This one was a little dull at times."

She winked at Alec and walked out of the office.

Frank Osborn, mouth open and eyes wide, looked down at the floor, staring dumbfounded at Janelle Lindsey's receding shadow.

Titles you have been waiting for...

Harlequin Gothic and Regency Romance Specials!

Regency Romance	Gothic Romance
DECEPTION SO AGREEABLE Mary Butler	RETURN TO SHADOW CREEK Helen B. Hicks
LADY ALICIA'S SECRET Rachel Cosgrove Payes	SHADOWS OVER BRIARCLIFF Marilyn Ross
THE COUNTRY GENTLEMAN Dinah Dean	THE BLUE HOUSE Dolores Holliday

Be sure not to miss these new and exciting stories

Harlequin Gothic and Regency Romance Specials!

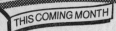

*Harlequin
Intrigue*

WHAT READERS SAY ABOUT HARLEQUIN INTRIGUE . . .

Fantastic! I am looking forward to reading other Intrigue books.

*P.W.O., Anderson, SC

This is the first Harlequin Intrigue I have read . . . I'm hooked.

*C.M., Toledo, OH

I really like the suspense . . . the twists and turns of the plot.

*L.E.L., Minneapolis, MN

I'm really enjoying your Harlequin Intrigue line . . . mystery and suspense mixed with a good love story.

*B.M., Denton, TX

*Names available on request.